HUNTER MORAN SAVES THE UNIVERSE

Patricia Reilly Giff

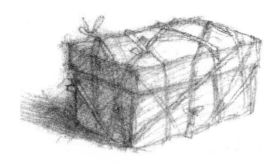

Holiday House / New York

Love to my sons,
Jim and Bill...
who deny any resemblance to Hunter and Zack

Text copyright © 2012 by Patricia Reilly Giff
Spot art copyright © 2012 by Chris Sheban
All Rights Reserved
HOLIDAY HOUSE is registered in the U.S. Patent and Trademark Office.
Printed and Bound in July 2012 at Maple Vail, York, PA, USA.
www.holidayhouse.com
First Edition
1 3 5 7 9 10 8 6 4 2

Library of Congress Cataloging-in-Publication Data
Giff, Patricia Reilly.
Hunter Moran saves the universe / Patricia Reilly Giff. — 1st ed.
p. cm.
Summary: While trying to hide an incriminating report card and dodge meddling
siblings, fifth-grade twins Hunter and Zack set out to save their town from a diabolical
dentist who is planning to blow it to smithereens.
ISBN 978-0-8234-1949-4 (hardcover)
[1. Twins—Fiction.   2. Brothers and sisters—Fiction.   3. Family life—Fiction.
4. Mystery and detective stories.   5. Humorous stories.]   I. Title.
PZ7.G3626Hu 2012
[Fic]—dc23
2012002969

YEE-HA!
THE FIRST DAY
OF SUMMER.

But...

Chapter 1

We have a major problem here. And to make matters worse, sneaking out the back door is like wading through a field of land mines.

Linny watches our every move. Because she's the oldest, she thinks she's the alpha dog.

William is painting a huge mural of worlds colliding on the hall wall. Globs of paint are everywhere...

...especially on our bare feet.

"Don't screw this up," I whisper to my twin brother, Zack, my sneakers slung over my shoulder.

"I won't, Hunter." He runs one finger across his throat, then slides through a dollop of midnight blue. He keeps his mouth shut, though, as the paint oozes up between his toes.

The stakes are high. One sound before we escape and we're stuck with our five-year-old brother, Steadman, for the rest of the morning. Steadman has a mouth that closes only to chomp down on chocolate bars and potato chips.

And yes, there's Mom's soft voice coming from the

kitchen. It's a little hard to hear her. Mary is screaming in there, banging a plate on her high chair. But basically what Mom's saying is "Linny, would you check on Hunter and Zack? Maybe they'll take Steadman—"

There's only one thing to do: duck into Mom's bill-paying room. It's so sacred that Linny will never guess we're there.

I open the door an inch at a time and go in on my knees, too smart to leave footprints. Behind me, Zack hops in on one foot. A good move, but it may be too late. Blue footprints follow him all the way down the hall.

We close the door behind us and sit on the floor, hardly breathing. Next door, St. Ursula's church bells clang a bunch of times. Ten o'clock, the day is wasting away.

Mom's bill-paying room is a mess, filled with papers and bills, pictures of Pop and the six of us, an empty birdcage from Petey, who turned up his claws before Mary was born last year, and Mom's cell phone, which is ringing like crazy, alerting the whole house.

Pick it up, which we're not supposed to do? Let it ring until we're deaf? Or until Mom comes in to see who it is?

There's something wrong with this phone anyway. The static is so bad, it sounds as if a typhoon is roaring in.

Linny's circling around outside. Any minute—

Zack reaches for the phone; he lies on top of it as if it's a grenade about to explode. The sound is hardly muffled. I reach under him for it. "Hello," I whisper.

"Agent Five here," a muffled voice says.

Who is he kidding? Or is it a she?

"Six here," I say, listening to what sounds like a hailstorm.

"Right on," I think the voice says. It sounds like he/she has swallowed a mouthful of stones.

I wonder if it's one of William's friends. Probably. They're all weird.

"The original missing from *S-T-U*," the voice says.

S-T-U. Ha. St. Ursula's Church next door. "Sure," I say.

I snicker into the phone. Zack covers his mouth.

The voice hesitates. "Dig . . ."

"What?" I say.

"Hunt—"

My name? Definitely a seventh-grade idiot in William's class. "Hunter?" I say to help things along. I add a few explosive sounds to go with the telephone typhoon.

The caller hesitates for the barest second. "Wrong number."

"You're right about that, buddy," I say.

The phone goes dead in my hands.

"So vat you tink about dat?" I say to Zack in a spy voice.

"I tink you'd better get out of Mom's bill-paying room." It's Linny, alpha dog, out in the hall.

"Arf," Zack says.

We're caught before we can even sneak out to the funeral.

Chapter 2

What a way to start the summer! Wind whooshing all over the place, rain spitting at us, a plane taking off from Sturgis Air Force Base with a grinding noise that could drive you crazy.

Heads together, Zack and I push the shopping cart out of the garage. We're on our way to Vinny's Vegetables and Much More. The cart eeks and squeaks along the driveway, on its way to falling apart, but we're stuck with a million things to carry home. You'd need a computer brain to remember it all.

The only thing that keeps this from complete boredom is a quick stop for the funeral.

"Some phone call," Zack says. "What do you think *the original* meant?"

Thoughts of Sister Appolonia pop into my head. There she was, a couple of weeks ago, looming over me and my fifth grade essay. She wore a tan suit that made her look like a cardboard refrigerator box. "Do you have one original thought in your head, Hunter Moran?" she asks.

Who could be original when the subject was building bridges in an urban community? Never mind *original*. I don't even know what *urban* means. No wonder I had to wing it.

I wing it now. "*The original* means..."

And then I give up.

"It could be anything," Zack, the thinker, says.

Next door, we pass St. Ursula's Church. Father Elmo has the sprinkler going even in the rain. When he isn't saving souls, he's saving the lawn.

"S-T-U," Zack mutters. "Something missing from the church?"

"Who knows?" I say.

Next we pass school. It's locked up tight, the windows bare and blank. Sister Appolonia is off for the summer. She announced that she was going to teach unfortunate children out west.

Unfortunate is right.

Diglio the dentist's house is on the corner. Diglio isn't into lawns; the patch in front looks like the Gobi desert. We're careful not to step on his weeds, though; Diglio is a yeller.

We cut across the street, pass Old Lady Campbell's house, and head toward Murdock Avenue.

"Our major problem is a little your fault," I tell Zack. I hold two fingers an inch apart to emphasize.

Zack bites his lip. He does that sometimes, teeth crunching one side and then the other. He doesn't answer; he doesn't have to. We can almost read each other's minds.

And what his mind says is that we shouldn't have tried to alter his report card in the first place, even though it was only to spare Mom's feelings.

7

We're talking about a simple change, an F to an A. One downward slash with a pen. The sad thing is that the rest of the card is great. Mostly As, with only a B in health. Zack messed up on how often you should brush your teeth. Sister Appolonia said with his approach, he'd have nothing but gums by the time he was thirteen.

No, this mark was for music appreciation.

Rain dribbles down the back of my neck. I hunch my head into my shoulders, thinking, as we eek and squeak along. Mom told Mrs. Wu, the librarian, that Zack's a musical genius. After all, he takes cello lessons from Old Lady Campbell.

Mom would be crushed by that F. We can't let that happen. Mom is the best.

But last night, we messed up the report card slash. Wrong color pen, then an eraser that drilled a hole through *Music Appreciation*.

We held the card out the window to catch a drop of rain and smush it up a little. We were left with a pockmarked report card. The only visible letter was that *F*.

"This whole thing just wore me out, Hunter," Zack said, holding his head.

"Never mind," I told him. "We'll have a ceremonial report card funeral."

That brightened him right up. And it's the main reason we're heading toward Vinny's Vegetables and Much More.

Sister Appolonia would be pleased. After all, she always says, "Use your common sense, boys, that is, if you have any!"

That's exactly what we're doing. We cut across the library lawn, heads down so Mrs. Wu doesn't see us. A mistake. I barrel into Old Lady Campbell, who drops her purse, a pile of books, and a couple of Kleenex. Right behind her is her dog, Fred. He's small, brown, and fuzzy, with breath that would knock you over; he just misses taking a chunk out of my leg.

"The library will open any minute," Old Lady Campbell says.

I pick up some of her stuff and glance at the sign over the door. Gigantic letters. NO DOGS ALLOWED.

Old Lady Campbell points to her huge shopping bag. "Fred just pops himself right in there," she says. "It works every time."

Mrs. Wu would have a heart attack if she knew.

Zack and I turn down Vinny's alley, moving fast; we pass under Diglio the dentist's office window, cringing at the sound of the shopping cart. It would be a mistake if Vinny realized we're heading toward his back door and his huge garbage pile. It's almost a mountain, filled with orange peels, banana crates, stringy bits of lettuce, and much more.

Zack has second thoughts. "How will I explain to Mom?" he begins.

"Don't worry," I say. "You never got an F before. No one will expect it. And you lose stuff all the time."

We hollow out a square of ground under some eggshells and in goes the report card. "Goodbye," I say in a hushed voice. "This is a sad loss for Sister Appolonia and St. Ursula's School."

I pay no attention to my buzzing cell phone. I know it's Linny. She's convinced we've stolen her skateboard. Zack's lost that, too. But we have enough to think about without skateboards.

"May you rest in peace, old friend," says Zack, leaning over the grave site.

We toss dirt over the whole thing, and that's when it happens. A torn piece of paper flies out of the shopping cart, almost as if it has wings. It loops around our heads before it nose-dives onto the grave and nestles there above the departed.

I bend over and pick it up with two fingers. Is it meant for us?

"What is it, Hunter?" Zack asks.

I read aloud: Bom/Twin. REVENGE!

I sink down on a cardboard carton.

What kind of craziness is this?

A note about twins?

Zack and me?

I kick at an empty cheese box.

What kind of revenge?

I gulp.

Wait a minute. What's the other thing Sister Appolonia always says? "You have the sad habit, Hunter Moran, of jumping to dubious conclusions."

Dubious. Whatever that means.

But there's only one conclusion here. Think about that phone call in Mom's room. Didn't the caller say "Hunt"?

Of course.

Zack looks at me in horror. "Someone may be after you, Hunter. Or both of us."

I straighten up, aiming for courage. We're thinking exactly the same thing. The call before? Wrong number. Right victim.

Zack turns the paper over. "There's a phone number here. Maybe it's the caller's. We'll call back, tell him we're innocent bystanders."

Zack knows he's talking nonsense. What we have to do is gather evidence and get the guy before he gets us.

And something else. Dig. Wasn't that on the phone, too?

Dr. Diglio, the dentist, I bet. Diglio with the beady eyes, the four strands of hair pasted over his baldy bean. Diglio, who hates me.

"You don't know that for sure," Zack says, reading my mind again.

But we both know I've crossed Diglio too many times. I wave the bottom of my T-shirt back and forth to get air. "It was an accident that I dinged his Acura with a rock."

Zack nods sympathetically. "You can hardly see it, with all the rest of the dings. That car is one lemon."

But there were other situations, too. My bicycle rutting up his desert front lawn, Diglio screaming as if it were the botanical garden.

My cell phone is vibrating like a plane going down. Linny never gives up. "What?"

11

"Don't get nasty," she says. "Where's the stuff from the store? Where's the milk for Mary? Someone drank it all."

"Want me to die of thirst?"

"No, just get back here before the summer is over."

I cover the phone. "Do you remember what else we were supposed to get?"

Zach's still squinting at the revenge message. "What do you think *Bom* means?"

"Cauliflower!" Linny screams into my ear. "Broccoli, two heads; carrots; dishwasher soap." She goes on and on. I close the phone, shutting off her voice with a satisfying snap, and squint over Zack's shoulder. *"Bomb,"* I say. "It stands for *bomb.*"

Zack hesitates. "Do you remember that movie? The one with the two kids and the bomb?"

How could I forget? I couldn't sleep for a week after I saw it. One kid was blasted away and half the neighborhood was gone. Actually, I look just like that kid, or what was left of him.

"Only pieces," Zack says.

What is all this about anyway?

The original is missing from S-T-U?

Original what?

But bomb? There's no doubt about it. It's all linked together, heading toward one thing.

Kaboom!

Zack frowns. "There goes the summer. We'll have to work this out before Diglio blows up Newfield."

And me, too.

Chapter 3

We take a different route home so we don't bore ourselves to death. We pass the town round, the park in the middle of town. Right in the center is a huge iron pot on a stand. It's Lester Tinwitty's original kettle, dinged worse than Diglio's Acura.

Lester dropped in by balloon, forged the kettle, and stayed to found the town. One by one, pioneers staggered in, starving, and whispering, "Soup, soup." All Lester had to do was stir up the pot.

I'm just glad I wasn't around then. I'd have eaten leaves or acorns instead of that soup, or even starved to death.

When we arrive home with the milk, beans, and two boxes of orange Jell-O, Linny is dancing up and down the front path. She grabs the bag out of the shopping cart and heads toward the house. "Mary is starving to death in there," she mutters.

Inside, it sounds like the roller coaster at Rye Beach. Mom is pacing up and down in the kitchen with Mary over her shoulder. Mary's face is eggplant purple from screaming.

Mom smiles at us. "Good work," she says as she pours milk into Mary's bottle with one hand.

"They forgot half the stuff," Linny says.

"Milk was the main thing." Mom looks like Sister Appolonia's picture of St. Dorothy.

Dorothy has a calm face, which is surprising because she's on her way to be devoured by lions in the Roman arena. It's also surprising that Sister Appolonia has that picture, since Dorothy went to her saintly death a couple of thousand years ago.

Zack and I go down the hall, sliding around William, who's working on his mural: a horrible view of outer space with worlds running amuck and crashing into each other. Mom thinks he's an artistic genius.

"Where are we going?" Zack asks me.

"Someplace private."

We sneak upstairs and detour into our bedroom to search for the huge flashlight Nana gave us last Christmas. We'd told her we needed it to see the night sky, which is ridiculous when you think of it, but Nana goes along with whatever we want.

We find it under the dresser with a few dust balls. Then we head into Linny's bedroom, which William has painted for her. It's a nightmare: volcanoes spewing lava onto the ceiling and buzzards flying over her dresser.

We inch our way behind her bed and slide open the door to the crawl space—all this with the utmost secrecy.

We don't want to alert Steadman, who is hammering something to pieces in the next bedroom.

You can't stand up entirely in the crawl space; it's probably over a hundred degrees, musty and dim; no one in his right mind would want to hang out in there. A perfect spot.

"Problem," Zack says.

I nod. Steadman is banging so close to the wall that it feels as if my head is going to come off.

"The telephone number," Zack says. "Shouldn't it have ten numbers?"

I aim the flashlight onto the paper and count. "Right."

Zack leans over my shoulder. "Only nine in this one. The end number is torn off."

I whisper the number: 393-555-144—and there it leaves off. "At the most we'll have to call nine people." I try not to shout over Steadman's noise. "We'll just keep adding numbers, zero to eight."

"Zero to nine," Zack says.

"No, that one's ours: five-five-five-one-four-four-nine."

"Genius." Zack gives me a high five. He looks down at the phone. "This thing is falling apart."

"Like everything else in this house," I say. "I think William stepped on it."

"Conked the Caller ID right out," Zack says. "Too bad." He punches in the first number: 555-1440. No answer.

Very suspicious, right from the start.

I try the next: 1441. But things are getting complicated.

Linny has just come into her bedroom. We hear her closing the door to muffle Steadman's noise.

We have to be ultraquiet. Linny gets furious when someone invades her space. And the crawl space is part of her bedroom. At least, that's what she says.

Someone answers the phone. I whisper "Hello," in a deep Pop-type voice.

"Is that you, Hunter?" someone asks.

It's Sarah Yulefski from my class. This is the worst possible thing. Last month Sarah told the whole fifth grade that I liked her. Liked her! She has braces over brown teeth and spits when she talks.

"No," I say. "This is Vinny's Vegetables and Much More. Your order is ready."

"Hunter?" she says. "Are you working there?"

I close the phone.

"Who's there?" Linny yells.

Zack and I don't move. We don't even breathe.

Linny doesn't move, either; she's afraid of kidnappers. After a minute, she rushes out of her room and slams the door behind her.

Steadman stops hammering; he clatters into Linny's room. "Just what we need," Zack says.

I crawl into Linny's bedroom, wiping cobwebs off the top of my head. "Hi, Steadman," I say.

"What are you doing in there?"

"Cleaning up the spiders. They could be poisonous."

"Great," he says. "I'll help."

"Cheech," Zack moans from the crawl space.

"I have a better idea," I say. "You could have ocean warfare with your men."

His eyes light up. Then he shakes his head. "We don't have any oceans around here."

"Follow me," I say.

I gather up a ton of his army men, his miniature tanks and ships, and take them into the bathroom. "We'll just fill the sink a bit," I tell him, "and you can slosh all these guys around." I dump everything into the sink, stick in the plug, and turn on the faucet.

"I'll be back soon," I say.

I race to the crawl space.

"Genius," Zack says, and hands me the phone so I can dial the next number. A quavery voice answers. It's Old Lady Campbell, Zack's cello teacher.

I press the End button quickly.

Then it's Zack's turn; he hits pay dirt. "It's Diglio," he whispers as a voice growls into the phone loud enough for the citizens of Uzbekistan to hear: "Dr. Diglio here."

He sounds so sinister, it almost scares me. You'd never believe he and Mom went to school together, that they even lived next door to each other growing up.

"Hello," Zack says in a voice that sounds like Whistling Ghost, Saturday Night Special.

"Olyushka!" Diglio says into the phone.

"Is that what you call the bomb, the one in the note?"

"Olyushka?" Diglio shouts. "What do you know about…"

Then all is static.

Zack and I stare at each other. And then Diglio's voice comes through again.

"Listen," he says. "I know you feel bad about their dying. But never mind, we'll be out of here soon. We'll forget about them. What do they do, anyway? Just hang around waiting to be fed."

Zack and I look at each other. Could he possibly be talking about us? All we do all summer is hang around. But how does he know about what we eat?

"Spying on us, that's how," Zack whispers.

Probably right in our kitchen window with binoculars. Horrible.

It makes me think of something. That's what we'll ask Nana to give us next Christmas, high-powered binoculars. If we're still alive, that is.

"Olyushka," Diglio begins.

"But why a bomb?" Zack cuts in. "Who are you working for? Is it Russia? North Korea? Antarctica?"

"A Moran kid!" Diglio snarls like Old Lady Campbell's dog, Fred. "You think I don't recognize your voice?"

"No." Zack chooses a name from our class at random. "It's Joseph Simiglia. I think I have the wrong number."

Diglio isn't fooled. "I see the number. I bet it's your cell phone."

We've made a fatal error. Of course he'd have Caller ID. Who'd dare step on his phone?

"Listen, you two." Diglio sounds as if he's coming through the phone at us. "Watch out that I don't see your father." He slams down the phone.

We sit there thinking; then we head for our bedroom.

"Can't even take a simple wrong number," Zack says innocently. "Something is wrong with Dr. Diglio."

We give each other another high five. That's exactly what we'll say if Diglio runs into Pop and tries to get us off the case.

But what is this all about? It's getting scary, really scary, if you ask me. The original missing from S-T-U, a bomb called Olyushka, my name—Hunt—and all of Newfield in jeopardy.

Chapter 4

Mom is the greatest. She can hit a ball as far as a major-league player. Well, almost. And she makes the best spaghetti in the world. It's her one great recipe. But she's a nervous wreck. She worries about break-ins, bacteria, and dirty fingernails.

"That's why we have to protect her," I tell Zack.

"Don't I know it, Hunter," he says, as inch by inch, we slide up our bedroom window. Even though two television programs are competing with each other downstairs and William is practicing his train whistle as he paints, Mom can still hear what's going on.

I poke my head out the window to test the air. At last the sun has come out. In a moment I'm going to jump.

From the window, the rope on Pop's flagpole whips around; the flag is long gone. "Breezy," I say, the wind tearing the words out of my mouth.

Zack licks his finger and sticks it out. "You're right."

We look down at the two-story drop into St. Ursula's garden. Right below is the fountain of St. Egbert, with a fringe of cement hair. Dribbles of water spew out from his hands, but not nearly enough to clean off the bird gunk.

"Don't want to hit that guy," Zack says.

No. We want to cross over to the half-dead sycamore tree and then onto St. Ursula's roof without taking a nose dive.

The roof is a humdinger: slippery gray slate with a steeple that pokes up forever. If we miss, there are no two ways about it. We'll slide down the slope, catapult into St. Eggie, and kill ourselves.

Mom will be a basket case, and Pop will be steaming mad.

I punch Zack's arm to toughen him up. We need strength. Zack punches me back. "Good thing we practiced, Hunter."

We've been working on flying skills. Sister Ramona, who's taught first grade at St. Ursula's for fifty years, also a nervous wreck, says practice makes perfect.

We glance at our beds, one on each side of the room. It's the worst mess. We've been jumping from one bed to the other, one desk to the other, over Zack's dusty cello case, then leaping up to grab the top of the open closet door.

"Not quite the same thing as trying for St. Ursula's roof," Zack says, reading my mind.

"It's for the good of the country," I remind him, not mentioning that my own life is at stake.

We're ready to go. Outside we'll have to balance

ourselves on a sill that's wide enough for a couple of toes. One thing we've learned is that you don't jump well from a standing position. We'll have to crouch down and spring into the air toward the tree like a pair of frogs.

"Let's get a move on before Mom gets up here," Zack says. "Poor Mom. She has enough on her mind with the rest of the kids without worrying about us."

"Especially William, who's painting the whole house," I say. "And Steadman, who leaves a trail of potato chips behind him as if he's Hansel heading toward the witch's house."

Mom deserves a break, we both agree.

We flip a coin to see who goes first. I win, or lose, depending on how you look at it. I scramble around until I'm outside the window. "Great view," I say, holding on to the sides with a death grip. "You can see into Diglio's yard and all the way to Tinwitty's man-sized soup kettle and the Star Union train station."

"Let's get this over with," Zack says.

"Right." I get into a crouching position so my chin almost touches my knees.

"Just pretend you're flying from my bed to yours," Zack says. "Nothing to it."

I squint at the steeple. I have to high-wire over to the tree, without the wire, then dive across to the steeple and straddle the roof point, in two smooth motions.

Old Lady Campbell is standing down below now, while Fred slurps water from St. Eggie's fountain, then scarfs down a half-eaten Pop-Tart from the path, wrapper and all. Old Lady Campbell herself is staring up at a plane going by from Sturgis Air Force Base. Her head is tilted so far back it looks as if she'll fall over any minute.

I have to concentrate. If I miss my jump, not only will I kill myself, but I'll smash her to smithereens.

And Fred, who begins to yap up at me.

It'll take Old Lady Campbell only a moment to see what's set the dog into a frenzy. There's not a minute to waste.

"*Olyushka*," I mutter. I sail out across St. Ursula's garden, over St. Eggie, grab a branch as thick as my arm, and hang there to catch my breath.

"Move!" Zack yells a little impatiently.

I kick back at the trunk with one foot, then let go.

And here comes the roof. Here comes the steeple.

I reach out and out and—

There it is, solid slate, just like we practiced.

I land harder than I expected, the breath knocked out of me, but I manage to wrap my arms around the steeple, straddle the roof, and get out of the way a second before Zack careens into me.

We crouch there, pleased with ourselves. Then we remember: the original missing from S-T-U, St. Ursula's Church. What could it be? Zack raises his hand to point.

It's a good thing Old Lady Campbell has left the scene, pulling Fred all the way. She doesn't see Steadman standing on the windowsill ready to jump.

Chapter 5

Steadman! Never mind his potato chip trails or his big mouth. He's funny and looks great when he gets cleaned up. I can't even stand to think of something happening to him.

"Go back!" I whisper-yell.

He teeters there, waving to Old Lady Campbell's back. "Hey, Fred," he calls to the dog.

Next to me, Zack is losing it. "Steadman!" he screams.

I know we're both thinking the same thing, how Steadman looks just after he wakes up, how excited he was on his birthday this year. He even shared his last piece of cake with me, a little gooey, mostly eaten, but still . . .

"Hang on, Steadman!" I yell.

The hall window goes up. Linny and her friend Becca poke their heads out. Becca is here again? She's the biggest know-it-all in the world.

Zack and I inch our way around the steeple so they can't see us.

They do see Steadman; their screech is loud enough to break our eardrums. Zack and I peer around the steeple as

Mom barrels out the back door, with Mary pinned to her jeans, a look of horror on her face.

And Steadman?

Steadman loses his balance but somehow manages to connect with the flagpole. He swings back and forth gently.

"Just like an orangutan," Zack says.

William comes out next. Mom always says he's the one with a head on his shoulders. He stands under the window, arms out. "Jump!" he yells to Steadman. "I'll catch you."

William may have a head on his shoulders, but he doesn't have too much in the brain department. He can't even catch a pop fly.

But Linny has brains. In two seconds she and Becca reach our bedroom. They lean out; Linny grabs one of Steadman's wrists and Becca the other one. They lug him inside an inch at a time, then slam down the window and lock it.

Something flits into my mind. Something about Steadman? Something important? Whatever it is, it flits right out again.

Old Lady Campbell disappears around the corner and William goes inside to spatter more paint on the hall wall. The 6:20 train comes into the station, while Mom sinks down on the doormat, crying, with Mary hanging off her shoulder. I can see Mom's lips moving. She's counting. She does that to calm herself. I can almost hear her. "Twenty-eight, twenty-nine, thirty..."

Poor Mom. It's all too much for her.

"Maybe we should do something for her," I whisper to Zack.

"We'll make our own beds," he said. "From now on. All we have to do is throw the quilts across the whole thing."

"She'll be thrilled," I say. "And at least we haven't been implicated in the Steadman situation."

Zack nods. "We'll be able to check out Dr. Diglio's house before he blows up Newfield."

I can't even bear to think of that.

We can see into Diglio's yard on the other side of St. Ursula's. The front may be a desert, but the back is a jungle. Hedges surround his fence, trees poke up here and there, and a tangle of butterfly bushes hides the windows. Probably a load of poison ivy, too.

It's a perfect spy backyard. You'd have to hack your way through to see what's going on in there. And that's what we might have to do. It's a good thing Pop has a hacksaw thrown in with his rusty tools in the garage.

"But where's Diglio?" Zack asks.

Like magic he appears out his back door, carrying a shovel. His head is hunched into his shoulders.

It's helpful that he doesn't look up. He walks to a tree, then bends over and begins to dig.

"Burying something," Zack breathes, as if I don't see exactly what he does. He snaps his fingers. "That thing we saw on TV? *Bombs Over*..."

"*Over Mars*. Tuesday night, eight o'clock. That's what

they did, kept the bomb in an underground tunnel until they were ready to use it. Then..."

"Olyushka," Zach says; he nudges me.

Pop is turning into our path from the train station, swinging his laptop in its orange case. Not only is Pop reliable, like Linny, he also has a head on his shoulders, like William, but once in a while it can be an irritable head. Zack and I will be confined to our bedroom forever if he catches us up here.

Diglio stops digging. Still bent over like a pretzel, he rubs the small of his thick back with one hand. "Arthritis like Nana," Zack says. "His government is really scraping the bottom of the barrel to hire him to blow up Newfield."

We don't dare peer around the steeple to see what Pop's up to. Pop not only looks like an eagle, his eyes are wicked sharp. We hear him, though. He's talking to Mom, who's telling him something.

"I know," Pop says in a calming voice. "They're barbarians."

"Good thing we're not involved in the Steadman caper," Zack says, barely moving his lips.

Mom is still talking. "And with Tinwitty Night coming up, I have to judge those soup entries to see which one is closest to Lester Tinwitty's secret recipe. It's all too much."

"You can say that again," Zack says, forgetting to whisper.

Pop looks up and we almost bury ourselves in the roof tiles.

But wait. Diglio's back door is opening slowly. We lean

27

forward. It's Mrs. Diglio. She teeters across the yard on killer high heels. Mrs. Diglio is his accomplice?

Any minute we'll uncover a whole nest of spies.

Mrs. Diglio carries a box in her hands. She holds it out as if she can't bear to touch it.

"What is it?" I ask. "What—"

"A bomb. Just like TV. They're burying it for now."

I nod slowly. Zack's a thinker, all right.

I wonder how powerful that bomb could be. I'm thinking of the St. Eggie statue with its tons of bird poop blasting out in a million soggy pieces. It'll hit our garden for sure. Pop will be fuming. He spends every weekend mucking around out back, planting, weeding, cutting, and screeching when he steps in one of Steadman's tunnels.

Now Mrs. Diglio bends down and carefully deposits the bomb in the hole.

"Olyushka," Dr. Diglio says.

I whisper, "We'll have to dismantle it. Good thing you can learn anything on the Internet."

Diglio takes a spy look around. The sun glints off his thick glasses. He looks up and he must see us. His mouth opens like a fat round O.

Zack and I sit entirely still, as if we're just a couple of extra slates connected to the roof. Diglio stares up at us, blinking hard, as if he can't believe what his eyes are telling him.

"You'd think he never saw two kids on a church roof

before," Zack says. We move around to the other side of the steeple to get his mind off us.

I hear Pop's voice. He's yelling, actually screeching.

Something comes to me in a flash. I have a horrible memory of the bathroom sink. I see water. I see Steadman's men floating around. I see that I haven't turned off the water. There's a lake in the bathroom. No, it's an ocean.

"Hunnnnn-terrrr!" Dad yells at the top of his lungs.

What next?

What's next is another problem. Linny has locked the window. How are we going to get back into the house?

Zack stares at the window, too.

It certainly is a problem.

.

Chapter 6

Zack nudges me. "How about the steeple?"

We raise ourselves up and crawl through a steeple window that has no glass. Inside, we hang next to two huge bells. If they clang, we'll be deaf for thirty years.

Below us is empty space all the way down. A rickety ladder leans against one wall. On the top rung, a pigeon perches on a messy nest.

"Hey, pidgie, pidgie," Zack says as we edge around her, reaching for a step. I've never been this close to a pigeon before. She looks at us suspiciously as we inch our way down. Zack does it one-handed to show me he could be an acrobat.

In two seconds we look like Steadman, with cobwebs in our hair and grit on our jeans. What's the matter with the people at St. Ursula's, anyway? The inside of the steeple hasn't been cleaned in years.

As we reach the main floor, Father Elmo comes out of the sacristy, surprised to see us. We try to look as holy as possible while Pop screams for us from our kitchen window.

Zack and I dip our fingers into the holy water fountain

and bless ourselves. I say a quick but earnest prayer, "Please let Pop calm down, and let us bring Diglio and his wife to justice, before Newfield goes kaboom."

We tiptoe out the door, dash around the side of the church, and stop at our kitchen door.

Inside, we slide into our seats at the table. Dinner is a nightmare. Pop goes on and on about the water and why don't we watch Steadman before he ruins the entire house.

Zack and I glance at each other. Ah, Pop thinks Steadman turned on the water. Nice. We're only the secondary criminals.

Luckily, Steadman doesn't defend himself. He's too busy dropping wads of spinach onto the floor under the table.

Mary has mush all over her face and doesn't stop banging her spoon on the high chair for a minute. The rest of us sit stone-still because Pop is into his "I work night and day and now I'll have to spend a month plastering the kitchen ceiling" speech.

I glance up. The ceiling has blisters. A couple have popped, and water from the upstairs sink drips onto the floor. I look down at my plate, a hamburger curled up around the edges, weedy-looking spinach, and cheese potatoes, the cheese a little hard.

I'd like to mention that I've become a vegetarian, excluding spinach, but I'd starve to death. Besides, Pop has veered into his "The boys belong in military school" speech.

Linny nods at Pop, then looks at us as if we've just escaped from Rikers Island prison.

William's head is buried in his shoulders. He's reading *The Lightning Thief* under the table.

But Steadman interrupts Pop, looking thrilled. "Can I wear a uniform?"

Zack and I begin to laugh, Zach spraying milk over the ketchup drowning his plate, and the two of us are sent to our room. Pop says he doesn't want to see us for the rest of the summer.

Upstairs Zack hands me half of one of his emergency Hershey bars. We need it for energy because what we're going to do next is more dangerous than anything we've attempted so far.

We have to break into Pop's laptop.

"You're a good guy," I tell Zack. He knows it's not because of sharing the candy. It's because he doesn't remind me that I dropped our laptop down the stairs during a fight with William.

Zack and I sit on our beds slowly chewing the Hershey bar. We have to wait until everything settles down in the kitchen. And that takes forever.

Dishes clang. Mary screams as she gets her bath and bed. At last Pop and Mom leave Linny in charge and take their nightly walk around Tinwitty's Kettle. After all, Mom is a descendant of Lester Tinwitty. That's why she judges the soup contest. A disgusting job, if you ask me.

It's a relief to have Mom and Pop gone. Pop will be happy by the time they get back, and we'll have the vital information from his computer on how to get rid of a bomb without blowing ourselves to kingdom come.

"Ready?" I ask Zack.

He crosses his fingers. We just have to find out where Pop hid the computer tonight.

"I'm ready," says Steadman from the doorway.

"Talk about spies," Zack says.

Steadman stands there holding a glass of chocolate milk. It's filled to the brim, which is a surprise, because a river of chocolate wends its way down his pajamas, joining the bunnies who are chasing carrots from sleeve to sleeve.

Steadman is the fifth kid in the family to wear those pajamas, but he's done the most damage to them. They're a mess of backyard dirt.

But what does he care? The legs are almost up to his knees. Soon the pajamas will be handed down to Mary and he'll get Zack's old ones with footballs all over them.

"Is Linny calling you, Steadman?" I ask, and Zack nods.

"What are we doing?" Steadman says.

"Linny probably has candy," I tell him.

"I know where Pop's laptop is," Steadman says.

"Where?" we say together.

"You're not supposed to—" Steadman begins.

Zack gives up his last emergency Hershey bar and Steadman leads us to the laptop. It's stashed in Pop's sock drawer under two thousand unmatched socks.

We drag it out and rush back to our room, slamming the

door behind us. We sink down against the bedroom door to keep it sealed tight as a tomb; Linny will be making her rounds any minute. I hold the computer on my lap. It's the key to saving Newfield, and even more important, the rest of the family. I press the On button.

One thing about Pop. He has limited imagination. We figure out his password in three tries. Helen, Mom's name.

The rest should have been easy. Zack was born knowing how to get the best out of a computer. He puts in *bomb* + *blow up* + *how to.*

"Not enough," I say. "Add *dismantle.*"

"Right," Zack says.

But Steadman leans over to wipe a drop of chocolate milk off the shift key. And that's when it happens. The entire glass of milk splats down on the keyboard and the screen goes dark.

My mouth turns as dry as Diglio's front lawn. But Zack is a good man in an emergency. He begins to work on the laptop first with the edge of his T-shirt and then with the bed quilt.

"I think Linny is calling me," Steadman says.

We move away from the door. "Don't tell—" I begin, but he's out of there.

Zack and I finish the cleanup job as best we can, zip the laptop into its orange case, and race it to Pop's sock drawer.

Back in our room, we sit on our beds trying to figure out what to do next. Zack's idea is to let Diglio bomb Newfield. "The two of us are finished anyway," he says, jerking his head toward Mom and Pop's bedroom.

But I think of Mom and poor little Mary, who smiles when she sees me; Mary, who has only two white teeth. I think of Steadman, who will never even get to kindergarten. Even William and Linny aren't so bad when you come right down to it. They'd save me if they could.

No, letting Diglio get away with bombing the town would be the coward's way out.

Instead, my idea is to dig up the bomb and throw ourselves on it to take the impact.

"We might even get a medal," Zack says, considering.

"Of course, we'd be gone," I say.

Zack bites his lower lip. "We'd have saved Newfield, though. They could put the medal right on top of the coffin."

I nod. "Pop would be so proud."

"I wouldn't go that far," Zack says.

Without another word, we dash outside to the garage and gather the equipment we'll need. We know what we have to do. We'll stay awake until the whole house is asleep, then head for Diglio's backyard.

.

Chapter 7

Outside, the front door slams shut. "We're back," Mom calls out to all of us. Tonight she sounds a little tired.

Usually Mom and Pop sit in the living room to watch the news of the world: boring stuff about potholes on Linden Boulevard, or the mayor running off with the city's money. But tonight we hear Pop's heavy footsteps coming up the stairs.

"Goodbye," I tell Zack, whose eyes are the size of pizzas. "This is the end of us."

The door flies open and Pop looms over us. "You're making your mother an old woman before her time," he says.

We hang our heads. The poor guy doesn't realize Mom is old already. She's at least thirty. She still looks pretty good, though.

Pop goes into his "I want you to turn over a new leaf immediately" speech. And immediately Zack asks what time it is.

Pop looks at him, openmouthed.

But I understand exactly what Zack is doing, even though

it's a little complicated. When Pop finds out we've ruined his laptop, Zack will be able to point out that the computer crash came before we were into the new-leaf phase.

Pop veers into his "You two have one last chance" speech. But this time there's a new ending. We'll be allowed to leave our bedroom if—

And it's a big if—

We take Steadman off Mom's hands. "Follow him around. Make sure he doesn't get into trouble," Pop says. "Tinwitty Night will be here before we know it. Lots of excitement."

Tinwitty Night, the most boring night in the history of the world. A thousand speeches. Disgusting soup. Hot dogs that taste as if they're actually stuffed with old dogs. But worse than that, Pop finds a million jobs for us to do beforehand.

Pop keeps going. "And most of all, set Steadman a good example. We have enough problems in this house as it is." He begins to mutter to himself, his hands up to his fore-head. "The house is falling apart. Leaks and garish murals all over—"

I wonder what *garish* means. But now Zack is making pizza eyes at me that fortunately Pop can't see.

For a moment I'm confused. Then I see Pop's shovel leaning against the wall with his wire cutters, hacksaw, and a loop of rope.

I hardly pay attention to the rest of Pop's talk. I'm trying to think how we'll explain what we're doing with that stuff. I decide to meet the whole thing head-on. "We'll build Steadman a playhouse," I say.

But for once Zack doesn't get it. "You mean take care of Steadman for the rest of the summer?" His voice is desperate.

I understand. Following Steadman around will make this the worst summer on record.

But Pop shakes his head. "No, not for the summer. For the rest of your lives." He slams out the door.

We listen to his footsteps pounding down the stairs. "It could have been worse," I say. "It could have been Mary."

Zack nods, kicking at the shovel, which hasn't been cleaned since we moved into the house. There's a trail of dirt leading from the door to the window.

We sit on our beds to wait forever, until at least eleven o'clock; then we pull some shirts and jeans out of our dresser drawers and stuff them under our quilts. "Like a pair of Tootsie Rolls," Zack says. "Sleeping Tootsie Rolls."

We saw that helpful trick in *Spider-Boy Returns*, Saturday morning, eleven-thirty.

We take a last look at our beds. We may never be back. It's a sad moment for both of us. But then I shake myself and grab the flashlight.

We just have to decide how we'll exit the house. Either way is dangerous: over St. Ursula's roof again in the dark, or down the hall without alerting Mom. Luckily Pop sleeps through anything, snoring like a rhinoceros.

But Zack brings up a third way. We both vote for that.

All we have to do is sneak into Steadman's room next door. Pop's rose trellis is right up against the window, so Zack and I can twirl down like a pair of roses going the wrong way. We've never tried that before.

"You have a head on your shoulders," I say. "Like William, who is painting garish murals."

Zack nods, proud of himself.

There's nothing left to do. We grab the shovel, rope, and cutters and tiptoe into Steadman's room. The moon is shining in on him and he looks peaceful lying there, his eyelashes down over his cheeks, a smear of chocolate on his chin, his thumb still in his mouth.

His eyes fly open. "Let's go, guys," he says.

"Go back to sleep," I whisper. "We're just checking to see if you're all right."

Like a miracle, he closes his eyes. We throw the equipment down on the lawn below. It makes more noise than we thought, and unfortunately, the shovel lands on the base of the rosebush.

We tackle the trellis. One thing I have to say about Pop. When he builds something, it stays built. About a thousand screws join the trellis to the side of the house. Hand under hand, we climb down, trying to avoid the rosebuds. Pop probably has every one of them counted.

Then, aside from a few nasty thorn scratches, we're outside, free. "Look back, Hunter," Zack says. The house is quiet, with only the hall light shining dimly through the windows.

"It was a great house," I say.

Zack bites his lip. "Maybe the bomb will be a dud. We'll be back in bed in an hour."

Neither one of us believes it.

Without a sound—"Utmost secrecy," we remind ourselves—we take giant steps around St. Ursula's Church. We try to avoid the sprinkler, which Father Elmo leaves on every night. He's in love with green grass.

We look toward Old Lady Campbell's house across the street. Every light is on in there. She must be on the lookout for burglars. So is Fred, who guards her property from her front porch. We move slowly, carefully. It would be a mistake to alert him.

A moment later, we stand outside Diglio's house. No lights, no dog, nothing to stop us. We climb over his fence and there we are in his backyard jungle.

We stand there, bent over a little, so we're not so obvious if Diglio looks out the window. He's probably lying there on the alert for one sound. Then he'll be outside, grabbing us, strangling . . .

"Which tree?" Zack asks.

I turn around, looking from one to the other. I like to look as if I know what I'm doing, so I do *eeny, meeny, miney, mo* in my mind, and point to the tree farthest away from the house.

Zack digs in with the shovel. I chop away with the cutters so we can get a better angle. I stack the branches carefully so we don't make a mess. After all, it's Diglio's yard, even if he's a spy. He may like that jungly effect.

Wrong tree.

Eeny, meeny, miney, mo.

I point to the second one, almost hoping I'll be wrong again.

"Listen, Hunter," Zack says. "My arm is going to fall off any minute."

I take the shovel. It's only fair.

At Old Lady Campbell's house, Fred begins to yap hysterically. I wonder how she stands that barking. We look toward Diglio's window, but all is well. The enemy sleeps like a baby. Wait, all isn't well after all. Something is moving outside Diglio's fence. We throw ourselves on his weeds. We hardly breathe.

"It's just your imagination," Zack says.

I nod, wondering if Fred has imagination, too.

When it's quiet, I begin to dig. I turn over the earth as quickly as I can. Too bad Diglio doesn't water once in a while. The ground is like cement.

I hear the clink. The shovel hits the box. And something—someone—climbs over the fence and drops into the yard. We hear the thud of feet.

We leave the bomb exactly where it is. We grab the tools and dash along Diglio's driveway, shoulders hunched. There's a killer loose in his backyard, and a bomb set to go off any minute.

It's the worst experience we've ever had.

Chapter 8

We don't stop until we reach no-man's-land, a narrow patch on the far side of our house. You can't see it from the street, so Pop puts no effort into mowing there. It's just as well; it's a great hiding place.

We throw the tools and ourselves over the cyclone fence and land in weeds up to our waist; we lie there, flat out, breathing in dirt and dandelions. The sound of crickets, or whatever they are, is loud in our ears.

We don't move for about a thousand hours.

"We're doomed," I say at last. "Someone else is after the bomb, or after us."

"Maybe we should work on an underground bomb shelter in here tomorrow," Zack says.

I don't answer. How much digging would it take to hold Mom, Pop, and the six of us? We'd have to keep going, tunnel under the whole house, and come up on the other side.

"Doomed," I say again, drawing the word out until it sounds like *Mysterious Voices*, Monday night, seven o'clock.

We sit up and lean against the side of the house. All is quiet now, even the crickets. Over our heads is a huge yellow moon that lights up Zack's face next to me.

He looks like a ghost.

We sit there, sucking on weeds that taste like chives.

"So who was it," Zack says, "who came into Diglio's yard?"

I shake my head. "This guy was spider fast. He climbed Diglio's fence in half a minute." I slap at a mosquito the size of a rocket ship.

"A real power ball," Zack says.

I don't want to think about that. Instead I go back over the phone calls, the clues. "Olyushka. Original missing from *S-T-U*. It's all very confusing."

"I forgot about the original," Zack says. "What kind of an original would Father Elmo have?"

"And what was that torn paper at Vinny's Vegetables and Much More?"

"We're missing a few things here. But one thing is sure. *Bom/Twin* can mean only two things. A bomb and..."

Zack sighs. "Twins. Us. A pair of innocent—"

"Not twins," I cut in. "Twin. Hunt. Me. I'm the innocent—"

I never get to finish.

Lights go on all over the house. The front door blasts open. I hear Pop's voice.

Heads down, we dig ourselves into the weeds again. A stone drills itself through my stomach, and Pop's hacksaw nearly cuts my ankle in two.

It's worth it. If Pop sees us . . .

He does, of course. His eyes are like lasers.

"What are you two doing out here?" he screams.

I slide out from under the hacksaw and stand up. It's a blessing he doesn't see his tools spread out in the weeds.

"The front door is wide open," he says as we climb back over the fence and head toward the house. "Every mosquito in Newfield is zooming down the hall, and Steadman is wandering around saying he can't find you."

I take a quick look at him.

"It's ten minutes after two," he says, holding his head. "And I have a meeting at nine in the morning."

Head down, I go up the front path. Zack is so close behind me I feel his breath on my neck.

"I can't get one night's decent sleep," Pop says, "without the two of you involved in one scheme or another."

We don't say anything. What can we say? That there's a bomb planted a couple of doors down, that I'm going to be toast, that Newfield may be a giant crater any minute?

He's not in the mood to hear all that.

"Go to bed!" he shouts. "Don't let me hear from you for the rest of the night."

Behind him, in the hall, stands Steadman, looking filthy as usual. "Hi, guys," he says. "Welcome home."

IT'S THE SECOND DAY OF SUMMER.

We're still...

Chapter 9

Alive!

I open my eyes with the sun on my face. I feel my arms and reach down to touch a bumpy scab on my knee. I'm still here. If Diglio weren't out to get me, I could relax. We could go back for the bomb and get rid of it without worrying so much. I try not to think about the other guy jumping over the fence last night.

Mary is singing in her crib, and Mom is downstairs frying bacon into cardboard.

Pop's footsteps come down the hall. "Don't forget about Steadman," he calls as he passes.

Steadman. It's always something.

Zach groans from the bed across the room. "Cello lesson this morning."

Zack, the musical genius, has another major problem: the concert at the town round on Tinwitty Night.

"Maybe it would have been better if the bomb had blown me to a Pacific atoll," he says.

I don't know what an atoll is, but I get the idea. He's had

a year to compose a cello piece for the concert, but all he has is *Do Re Mi Mi Mi*. Or something like that. And the cello is in very bad shape. Ruined, as a matter of fact.

That reminds me of Pop, on his way to the station, swinging his computer case, unaware that the innards are sloshing back and forth with every step he takes.

"What's going to happen when Pop opens the laptop?" Zack asks, reading my mind again.

"Don't think about it. Think about the cello instead."

"Maybe I shouldn't have bashed it over William's head after all," he says.

"What's done is done. You just have to get a good story together for Old Lady Campbell."

We shake our heads together. She's wicked old, with a wrinkled face, and she hobbles around on a cane, but our story can't be…what's that Sister Appolonia word…*dubious.*

"Throw yourself on her mercy," I say. "Maybe she won't tell."

The bedroom door bangs open. Steadman is standing there. He's really a mess this morning. The only thing about him that's clean is his sucking thumb. He throws himself on my bed. "It smells down there in the kitchen," he says.

The first of the soup entries must have arrived.

Steadman leans up on his elbow. "Mom wants to see you."

Now what? "We're on our way down," I say.

"Want to hang out today, Steadman?" Zack asks.

Steadman scratches one muddy knee. "You have a cello lesson."

"You can wait with Hunter. I won't be as long as usual." Zack looks relieved. It's the end of cello lessons forever. He just has to tell Old Lady Campbell. Somehow.

"Nothing to it," I tell Zack, to bolster him up.

Steadman is thinking. "Fred loves me. He's always slobbering over me." He looks up at the ceiling, happy about Fred's slobbering.

But then he shakes his head. "Nah, I have to stay home. I have some buried treasure to look at."

Zack and I shrug at each other. We can't force him.

"Besides, Pop won't be home for hours," Zack says. "What can Steadman possibly do while we're gone?"

One problem solved.

But breakfast is something we hadn't expected. Mom is holding an investigation. We sit at the table chomping down the bacon, then chewing on the granola Nana sends every month to keep us fit. It's rock-hard and the crunch sounds like the garbage truck thundering down Murdock Avenue. At the same time, I try not to breathe in the soup that's simmering on the stove.

"This didn't just happen by itself." Mom points toward the trellis outside the window.

I take a look. Usually it looks great, with roses all over

it. Today it doesn't look so hot. "Dead as a doornail," I say through a chunk of granola.

"How did it get that way?" Mom's voice has an edge.

"Somebody killed it," William, with a head on his shoulders, says.

Zack and I realize at the same moment. Last night. The climb. The shovel must have sheared off the root. Zack does that teeth-on-the-lip thing, one side to the other. His eyes slide away from mine. "Not somebody. Some..." He hesitates. "Thing?"

I notice a long scratch down the side of his cheek. It must have come from the rosebush.

Zack opens his mouth. He's confessing?

But no.

"Blight kills bushes," Zack says. "And fungus." He raises his hand to his cheek, as if he's thinking. He's trying to hide the scratch. "It's probably an army of—"

"Moles?" I say. The perfect answer. Pop has been having a war with moles for years. The moles always win.

Zack's sneakers connect with mine under the table. A foot low five.

Mom taps her spoon against her lips, and we wait.

"Maybe," she says, and then, "Climbing the trellis is not a good thing."

"You could break your neck." I try to sound wise and fearful at the same time.

Everyone is staring at us. A dangerous moment.

"Well…" Zack pushes back his chair. "Time for cello. I'll just get…" He runs upstairs for the empty case.

"I'll go with Zack." I slide out of my seat, heading for safety. "I like to listen to the music."

William snickers. He still has a bump on his head from where the cello connected. Besides, he saw us burying the cello at the back of the yard two days ago. Zack and I gave it a great send-off, a funeral with a twenty-one-gun salute. Without the guns, of course.

Linny shakes her head at Mom. Then Zack and I are off.

"Are you going to tell Old Lady Campbell the exact truth?" I ask him.

"Don't talk," he says. "I'm trying to think."

We head over there, and don't even have to knock on her door. Fred explodes down the hallway; his eyes bulge and I can count his canines. He's ready for a quick meal. Old Lady Campbell drags him by the collar and wrestles him into a bedroom as he looks back, snarling. She slams the door, just missing his muzzle.

"Fred gets a little overexcited sometimes." She smiles at us with yellow teeth.

I remind myself to brush and floss so my own teeth don't look like hers when I'm an old man.

With a bony hand on Zack's shoulder, she guides him into her studio. I sink into a kitchen chair to wait. Over my head, the curtains are sheared off halfway up. "Fred loves the taste of lace," Old Lady Campbell told us once.

I sit there, dying of boredom. I slide open a drawer. Knives, forks, and a bottle of Feel Like New tablets, *four a day for four months*. The pills are the size of elephants galloping though the rain forest... or wherever they gallop.

Yuck.

The next drawer is filled with pictures that might have been taken a hundred years ago. Looking at them makes me dizzy. Upside-down mountains. Tilted houses. And is the one on top Old Lady Campbell in goggles? Piloting a plane? Brown hair streaming out behind her?

I tilt my own head. Maybe that was it. She was taking pictures of herself and the rest of the world from the plane.

I'm right. The next bunch of pictures are all of planes, some just the wings, some just the tails, one just the wheels.

Cheech! What a waste of time.

I breathe in. Something is bubbling along on her stove. It's mostly green with some yellowish lumps here and there.

Let me guess. She's going to enter the soup contest.

There's a crumb cake on the table. I pick a fat lump off the top. Delicious, but obvious. It leaves a blank space in the middle of the cake. I stare at it, turning the plate in different directions.

What a trying summer this is. A spy after me with a bomb, Steadman, the trellis, and now this. It's almost too much. Oh, and don't let me forget Pop's laptop.

I poke at the lumps around the space, trying to edge them closer together, but it only disturbs the white sugar.

Now, in addition to the space, a dark spot surrounds it, looking like a bomb crater.

Something squirrels into my mind. But who can think with Fred barking like a maniac in the bedroom and a plane from Sturgis Air Force Base zooming overhead, its engine loud enough to rattle the dishes?

Carefully, I edge a crumb off the edge of the cake. "Bom/Twin," I whisper, and drop it into the crater.

Not bad.

Notes are sawing in the studio. How could that be? It comes to me in a flash. Old Lady Campbell is going to lend Zack a cello. He must be devastated.

I reach into the drawer, slide out a wicked knife, and whittle a half-inch away from all four sides of the cake. Precisely. Like a surgeon amputating someone's arms and legs. I chew thoughtfully.

"Good job," I hear Old Lady Campbell telling Zack.

"Good job," I say to what's left of the crumb cake.

But why am I uneasy?

I have a lot to be uneasy about. And the very worst is Diglio, with a bomb unburied in his backyard.

Bomb. I stand up. The chair tips over and bangs against the refrigerator. I rush down the hall—past the bedroom with Fred in a frenzy—and slam open the studio door.

"We have to go home right now," I tell Zack.

In an instant, Zack catches on. "Hunter's had some problems lately," he says.

"What's the problem?" Old Lady Campbell yells over Fred's noise.

"It's a sickness."

I can hardly talk, with what's facing us at home. "It's Olyushka disease," I manage.

"Rare," Zack says. "We have to get him into bed."

We race down the hall. Behind us, Old Lady Campbell leans on her cane. "I may be old, but I'm not daft," she mutters.

Whatever that means.

"Take the cello," she calls out the door after us. "Be careful with it. It was mine when I was ten years old."

An antique.

Outside, I blurt out, "Danger of the worst kind."

We dash across St. Ursula's front lawn, get soaked in the sprinkler, and head for our kitchen door.

Chapter 10

Mom is in the backyard with Mary, pruning the rosebush. "Maybe I can save it yet," she says.

"Great." I don't stop.

"Lunch sandwiches on the kitchen table." She wipes her forehead. "How was the lesson?"

"Learning Bach," Zack says.

I'm almost dancing up and down on the back steps as he launches into Bach's life story.

He's probably making half of it up.

At last we skitter into the kitchen and grab a pair of tuna fish sandwiches to take with us. Linny blocks the hallway. Not only is she reliable, she has reliably big ears. "I heard Pop tell you to watch Steadman," she says.

Becca is right behind her, ready to stick her nose into our business. "What are they up to now?" she says.

"Let us pass," I tell them desperately.

Linny puts her hands on her hips. "Now I'm the one who's been stuck—"

"We're going up to him right this minute."

Linny pokes her skinny finger in my face. "Good luck. He's locked in his bedroom."

"And who knows what he's up to," Becca adds.

"Out of the way," Zack says, "or get bopped in the beano."

They step aside and we dash upstairs.

"Remember last night," I ask Zack when we reach the top, "someone jumped over the fence into Diglio's yard?"

"How could I forget?" But then he sees where I'm going with this. His eyes widen. "You think it was Steadman?" he sputters. "Out in the middle of the night with a buried bomb? By himself in Diglio's yard?"

"Not by himself. We were there."

Zack breathes in. "He went out the front door."

"And he was mud filthy—" I begin.

"And ready to play with buried treasure." Zack leaves tooth marks in his lower lip. "Yeow! The bomb! We're all going to the stratosphere."

Linny's right as usual. Steadman's door is locked. I rattle the knob.

"Let us in," Zack says, nose to the crack.

"What's the password?" Steadman asks.

He does this every time. It could be anything.

"Tinwitty Night," I say through a mouthful of tuna fish.

"Soup," Zack says.

Steadman's laughing. "Not even close."

"No time to waste," I tell Zack.

Zack nods. "Let's go back to our bedroom."

"We'll eat all that candy." My voice is loud.

"I'm coming." Steadman fumbles with the door.

We hear clicks and clacks and rattles.

"It won't open." He sounds a little frantic.

I crouch down, trying to look through the keyhole. "Just jiggle the thing again."

He jiggles. Nothing happens.

"Listen, Steadman, what does your buried treasure look like?" Zack asks.

Steadman bangs on the door. "I have to get out of here."

"Don't worry," I say.

Zack and I look at each other. We're worried, all right. "Out the window again," he says.

But this time it's a different route. We race up the attic stairs, jump over a pile of old clothes, push aside our long-dead great-grandfather's picture in what looks like gray underwear, and head for the window. Down below, Mom is still pruning, her shears flashing. Mary's asleep on the grass. William sits in back on the cello's grave.

"Maybe the bomb won't spread out as far as the yard," Zack says. "The rest of the family might be saved."

"Are you kidding? St. Ursula's will be a pile of rubble. And forget about Father Elmo's lawn."

"Fred, too," Zack says, with some satisfaction.

I push up the window and release a thousand flies outside.

Mom looks up and I duck back. "You'll have to go down there," I whisper. "Talk about Bach or someone."

Zack doesn't waste a moment. He clatters down the stairs. I don't waste a moment, either. By the time he's telling Mom about Bach's terrible bout with blindness, I'm out the window backward, reaching for Steadman's sill with my feet. It's terrifying. I don't want to think what will happen if I miss. But we've done this before.

Steadman opens his window and, moving an inch at a time, I finally tumble inside.

I hold out my hand. "Where's the treasure?"

"Where's the candy?"

I reach into my pocket. All I have is a linty Life Saver. I hold it out. I see the black box, trailing dirt and tied up with a rope that has about a thousand knots. It waits for us, like a giant squid ready to destroy us.

I have to think fast.

The weedy woods are only a trek across the street, past the driveway of the empty house, and—

I have a better idea. Lester Tinwitty's soup kettle on the town round! That baby is so thick it'll take the blast easily. Lester would be proud of me.

I grab the box by the rope with one hand, unlock the door and drag Steadman down the stairs with the other.

"Taking Steadman to the park, Mom," I call over my shoulder.

Zack catches up, and we dash along Murdock Avenue until we reach the town round. Already the stores have put up flags in their windows.

And there it is, the enormous black soup kettle looming up in front of us. We wend our way down the path; up ahead Old Lady Campbell is giving Fred his daily outing.

"Stay down here with Zack, Steadman," I say. "I'll climb up to the kettle."

He opens his mouth, but I pay no attention. I climb the six steps slowly, holding the box out in front of me, like *Son of Dracula*, Wednesday night, seven-thirty. I look back over my shoulder. I can see Diglio's, St. Ursula's, and the garbage cans in front of our house.

A plane from Sturgis Air Force Base zooms overhead, and Steadman yells, "What are you doing with my treasure?"

I don't answer. The cover is opened a couple of inches. Not enough. I'll need both hands for this. It's heavy as lead. I put the box down and begin to push. After a minute or two of strongman effort, I raise myself up and peer into Lester's Kettle. It's soup, all right. Candy wrappers, dead flies, and a few leaves float around in a muck of leftover rain. Lester Tinwitty would be horrified.

Steadman starts up the stairs.

"Stand back," I say, but before I can even add "Bombs

away," there's something else to worry about. A black-and-white patrol car has just pulled up in front of our house. Two cops with nightsticks bristling from their belts are heading up our front path.

Before I can drop the bomb into the pot, Steadman grabs it and runs, the bomb ticking its life away in his arms.

Chapter 11

"Come back!" I yell to Steadman, who zigzags across the street. He races through Father Elmo's sprinkler and disappears around the side of the church.

We gallop toward the church, too, glancing back at the patrol car.

Zack reads my mind. "Let William with the head on his shoulders take care of the cops," he says breathlessly.

But Linny is heading our way. *"Hunter! Zack!"* she screeches. You'd think she'd be worried about the cops hauling us off.

Steadman comes back, the bomb gone. Any minute, St. Eggie's head is going to blast off all over Newfield.

Linny doesn't stop with her screaming.

Zack and I duck behind a half-dead tree and peer out at the cops who are standing on our front step.

"Are they after you?" Steadman asks.

I drag him behind the tree with us. "We'll have to hide until all this blows over," I say.

"Or everything blows up," Zack whispers.

"What do you think they've got us for?" I ask.

"Pop turned us in because of the laptop." Zack presses his forehead against the tree trunk. "Or maybe Diglio is having us arrested for trespassing."

I shake my head. "No, Diglio knows we'd reveal everything during an interrogation."

Zack nods thoughtfully. "Especially about the bomb."

"A bomb?" Steadman says.

"No, don't worry," Zack tells him. "It's a new kind of candy. Bomb—"

"Bombalusa Nut Bar," I say.

Steadman frowns. He looks at us with some suspicion.

"Really," I say. "It's delicious."

But Zack is still whispering. "Diglio will have some story. He's crafty. We'll end up as the bad guys in prison, drinking out of tin cups and wearing those striped outfits."

"At least you won't have to take cello lessons," I say, trying for comfort.

Steadman's lower lip trembles. "I have to sleep in my own bed, with my own blanket. And my own treasure." He takes off running, back around the side of the church.

We can't follow, not yet. One of the cops is looking in our direction as Linny yells her lungs out.

At last, the cop turns toward the door. We wait for a second; then, heads down, we go after Steadman, but he's nowhere in sight.

"Maybe he circled around the other side of the church," Zack says. "On his way to Murdock Avenue."

Zack and I race after him, narrowly avoiding Old Lady Campbell on the sidewalk, and Fred, who lets out a frothy growl. "Sorry, Old...Mrs. Campbell!" I yell over my shoulder.

"Practice for the concert, Zack!" she yells back.

Steadman's probably ducked into Vinny's Vegetables and Much More. Zack and I barrel inside, up one aisle and down another. And there's Steadman, hiding behind a cut-out of a sparkly-toothed woman with a tube of toothpaste.

How nice that toothpaste tube is. Ours is always dented in the middle, with white stuff stuck to the top. But I have more important things to think about. Steadman sits there, the bomb cradled in one arm and his thumb in his mouth.

I crouch down next to him. "You're not going to prison. You have to be ten years old."

"*You're* going to prison, then, right?"

"I'll text you all the time."

Steadman bursts into tears. "What good is that? I still can't read."

"I'll draw pictures," Zack says. "And send them."

"Your drawing is horrible." He begins to wail. "You're going to prison, too? I'll be stuck with Linny and William."

"Don't forget Mary," I say. "You love Mary. We all love Mary."

Steadman's lower lip sticks out a mile. "What good is Mary? All she does is bang spoons around."

This is going nowhere. I wrestle the box out of his hands and edge it behind a pile of sardine cans; I kick at the end of the rope so that's hidden too. "We're hiding your treasure," I tell Steadman. "Keeping it safe."

The eyes of the sardines that are painted on the cans glare at me. They don't want to be blown to bits, either.

Steadman thinks about it. "I guess." But he isn't finished. "I'll probably be captured by Diglio."

Zack and I stare at him. "How do you know about that?" I say at last.

Vinny comes down the aisle. He thinks he's the king of the supermarket world. "You guys again." He points with his thumb. "Out!"

We step around him and head for the door. All the while he's muttering, "Those Moran kids could drive you crazy."

Then we're out in the sunshine.

But Zack stops dead. "Where's the bomb?"

I slap my head. "Hanging out with the sardines."

We sneak back inside and dash down the aisle to the toothpaste display, but the bomb is gone. Vinny with his X-ray eyes probably threw it in his garbage dump out back.

Too bad for Vinny.

But now we have to face the police. We head back to the house. Linny stands at the corner, hands on her hips.

"Where have you been?" she screams. "I thought you were kidnapped. It's a good thing Mom wasn't here. She would have had a heart attack."

"Does Linny know how to talk in a normal voice?" I ask Zack, loud enough for her to hear.

Becca shakes her head. "How do you put up with them?" she asks.

"Linny's throat will be ruined with all that screeching," Zack says. "The swelling may cut off her windpipe."

Linny's mouth snaps shut. Along with kidnappers, she's afraid of choking to death. From the corner of my eye, I see the flashing lights on the patrol car throw a Christmas-red glow over the trees. The cops are talking to William on our front steps.

"Do you know what the police want?" I ask.

"Probably to lock kids like you in jail and throw away the key," Linny says.

Steadman opens his mouth so wide you can see his back teeth covered in chocolate. He begins to scream.

"Now see what you've done," Zack tells Linny.

She leans over and gives Steadman a hug. "Not you. You're a great guy."

Steadman screams on.

"It's terrifying," Linny says over Steadman's head. "William told me before. Pop called. His assistant spent the morning fixing his computer. It was covered with a strange liquid. The assistant said someone probably hacked into it. Maybe a terrorist who's messing around with making a hydrogen bomb and blowing up the world."

A terrorist! The pressure is off. "Yee-ha!"

Linny looks at me as if I've lost my mind. But Zack is worried. "Is that why the police are here?" he asks.

"Don't be silly." Linny looks back toward the cops. "They're talking about Tinwitty Night, how everyone has to help out. Donate money for the big prize, a trip to the Ozark Mountains. They say everyone will be lucky to slurp up some of that winning soup." She wrinkles her nose. "Gross."

It's probably the first time Linny and I have ever agreed on anything. Last year someone added a possum tail to the mix. It makes me shiver to think of it.

Zack still looks uneasy. He's thinking about the Tinwitty concert, I bet. I don't blame him. I'd be ready to throw myself in the soup pot if I had to compose a cello piece in two days.

The policemen come down the front path. They don't bother with us, a bunch of innocent kids, one of them screaming so loud you can't even hear yourself think.

But Steadman draws in a mighty breath. When he lets it out, he calls to the cops. "I can help you. I know all about the bomb."

Chapter 12

"Heh, heh." Zack's laugh sounds fake, almost like the Joker's in *Batman*.

The cops turn to stare at Steadman.

"That's my little brother." I put my arm around Steadman and shake my head wisely, even though my knees are knocking together. "He can't even read yet. Not a word."

Steadman opens his mouth. I pretend I'm wiping some of the dirt off his mouth.

But a miracle occurs: a crackling sound. One of the cops raises a hand for quiet. It's their radio. More important things are going on than someone trying to blow up the world. They take off running and jump into the patrol car. With lights still flashing, they hit the road.

I stare down at Steadman. He's clueless about what he's put us through. He's actually grinning up at me with those chocolate-covered teeth. I have a terrible realization that he must have stolen a Hershey bar from Vinny's Vegetables and More.

My brother, a thief. What will this do to Mom?

Linny opens her mouth. "Another thing. Do you know what I found? Do you know—"

Zack nudges me. We have no time to listen to her.

"On the back porch," she says. "About a hundred concert tickets. All gunked together with hard candy."

"They're just not dependable," Becca says, her nose twitching like a rabbit's.

Zack looks as if he's going into shock.

"It's a wonder the rain didn't get them." Linny shakes her head.

Steadman and I trot around the back after Zack and sink down on the step.

Zack holds his head. "I was supposed to sell them for the concert."

Some concert, with no audience.

Zack begins to pull the tickets apart and holds one up. A lemon lollipop stick is stuck to the edge.

"Oh yeah," Steadman says. "That's where I left that lollipop."

"I can't stand much more of this," Zack says. "Danger is one thing, but Steadman—"

"What's dangerous?" Steadman asks.

"Stealing chocolate from Vinny's Vegetables," I say.

"I just opened the candy bar the tiniest bit," Steadman says. "I bit off an edge and put the rest right back."

How gross is that?

"See what I mean?" Zack says.

"Listen," I say. "There's no time to waste. We'll find the—" I break off, looking at Steadman. "It's probably sitting on Vinny's garbage pile. We'll bury it, then sell the tickets." I think about it. "You can say they're that way on purpose. You're composing—"

Zack gives me a high five. "The Sticky Symphony."

On the way to Vinny's, we swing Steadman between us like a flying gorilla. But bad news. We can't get down Vinny's alley. The supermarket king has locked the gate.

"Serves him right," Zack says. "Blown to kingdom come because he's too mean to let anyone near his garbage."

"We'll figure it all out," I say. "Don't worry."

Zack takes a breath. "In the meantime, let's get these tickets going."

We zigzag down the block and bang on the first door. Who answers? Our luck. Sarah Yulefski, with braces and brown teeth. Yulefski, who thinks I'm in love with her.

Zack moves in front of me. "We're selling tickets to the concert. How many would you like to buy? Five? Seven?"

"How about twelve?" Steadman puts in.

Sarah smiles her terrible smile at me. "Did you forget? I'm *in* the concert. I'm playing a violin masterpiece I composed myself." She sighs. "You were supposed to sell those tickets months ago. I sold forty myself."

How could that be? Who in his right mind would buy a

ticket to hear Zack and Sarah Yulefski? And right now Sarah gives me a Miss American Beauty Queen smile with corn-flakes stuck to her braces.

I step back and nearly fall off her steps. And Steadman is right there with his mouth. "Some set of choppers you have," he tells her.

She smirks at him. "Dr. Diglio's work. I just got back from his office on Murdock Avenue. He had to fit me in. He's leaving right after Tinwitty Night."

It hits me. Diglio will skip town just before the bomb detonates.

The clock is ticking away.

"I know," Steadman says.

Steadman's reading my mind? It's very discouraging.

"We'd better get over to Diglio's house right away," Zack says. "See what's going on there."

And that's what we do.

But all is eerily still at Diglio's. His dinged Acura isn't in the driveway, and today's newspaper is still on the front path.

"What does that tell you?" Zack says.

"That we're too late," I say. "He's moved on with the original, whatever that is. Right to ..." We don't even know where. How could we possibly follow him?

"Nah," Steadman says. "It tells me that he's still at his office."

Zack looks as if he's going to explode. He makes a zipper

with his pointer finger and his thumb and runs it across his mouth. "When I do this, stop talking."

Steadman pays no attention. He speeds up the path ahead of us. "Come on," he calls. "Let's look in the window."

"Let him fend for himself for two minutes," I say, and we tiptoe into Diglio's backyard jungle. We look carefully, crawling up and down the yard, but Diglio is too smart to leave any clues in his weeds. Then—

My heart almost stops. Inside the house, someone is speaking. We dive down into the bushes, landing on sticks that are as sharp as swords. What sacrifices we're making for the good of the country.

I raise my head an inch as the back door opens. It actually creaks like the chiller stuff on TV. And there's Mrs. Diglio in a black outfit with a bunch of lace and dagger-sharp heels. She looks highly dangerous.

Zack gasps and grabs my wrist.

Next to Mrs. Diglio, with some kind of pie thing stuffed in his mouth, is Steadman.

Steadman!

And he's pointing right at us.

Steadman walks down the steps with Diglio's accomplice. "Hunter," he calls. "Zack. Good news."

There's no hiding ourselves. Mrs. Diglio peers at us through diamond-studded glasses.

Steadman goes on. "Mrs. Diglio isn't a spy."

We stand up and wipe the mud off our jeans. "Heh, heh," Zack says. "Of course not."

"We were…" I wave my hand, trying to think. Why would we be hiding in her jungle? And then it comes to me: "…wondering if you'd like to buy a concert ticket."

"Come in," she says.

There's danger, staring us right in the face. But Mrs. Diglio has a firm grip on Steadman's arm. We have no choice. We follow her into her kitchen, the middle of her web.

It's very disappointing, just an ordinary kitchen, except for killer-vine wallpaper. What isn't ordinary is a fish tank filled with greenish water. If there are fish in there, they're well hidden. I don't even glimpse a fin or a tail. No, wait, there's something sliding along on the bottom. A slug? A snail? Strange.

And another thing. Locks bristle from the inside of the door and iron bars crisscross the windows. It's a regular Hansel and Gretel prison.

Will we ever get out of there alive?

Mrs. Diglio puts a plate of spy cookies in front of us and pours lemonade. She sees me staring at the door. "New locks," she says. "There are maniacs all over the place. Frightening."

"It certainly is," I say, wishing Pop would fix the lock on our door. He's very careless about things like that.

"They climb over the fence." Mrs. Diglio leans forward. "They've cut up my bushes, put them in piles."

Zack stares at me. What is he trying to say? And then it comes to me. We're the maniacs she's talking about. Imagine. Spies like the Diglios worrying about things like that.

I glance down at the pad in front of me. Mrs. Diglio has terrible handwriting, even for a spy. There's a pile of *Z*s and *X*s; she may have added a new letter to the alphabet.

I try to read without her noticing. *Nead*, it begins. Then a list. *Alarm cluck, big hands to see in dark. Earploogs to miffle sound.*

Miffle? Muffle the sound of a bomb going off as they speed away? And what about that alarm cluck? Don't they use clocks as timers for bombs? Didn't I see that on some program? Maybe *Death on Planet X*, Thursday night, nine o'clock?

I snap my fingers trying to think. Then I realize everyone is staring at me. I go *mmm, mmm* with my mouth filled with cookie, as Mrs. Diglio talks about the neighborhood being overrun with noot cases.

Whatever that means.

There's more. All strange things. And at the bottom . . .

At the bottom . . .

Is *Olyushka*!

That's it. We're toast.

Mrs. Diglio moves as fast as an iguana. She scoops up the pad and puts it in a drawer. Then she clears her throat, so I look up quickly, innocently. Steadman's mouth is full and wide open. It's a cement mixer in there. I give him the zipped-lip signal, and the cement mixer snaps shut.

He takes that moment to spill his lemonade across the plate of cookies, the plastic tablecloth, the chair, the floor, and himself, of course.

Zack and I jump out of the way, saying, "Sorry."

Then, like a St. Dorothy miracle, I hear Linny's screechy voice in the background. "Get in the house, Hunter! Zack! It's time to eat!"

Perfect.

"We have to go," Zack says, his eyes the size of Lester's soup kettle.

To our great relief, Mrs. Diglio opens her forty locks and we head out toward freedom.

"Wait!" she yells, but we don't stop. Of course not.

"You forgot," she goes on. "The concert tickets."

"We'll be back," Zack shouts.

But that's not going to happen, we both know that. It's a miracle we've escaped with our lives.

HERE WE ARE— DAY THREE OF SUMMER.

It's hot, sticky, and time is running out....

Chapter 13

Breakfast may never be over. Pop keeps talking about computer hackers ruining the world.

Zack and I agree.

He's also a little irritable, maybe because drops of water from the ceiling plink and plunk down on his head.

He leaves for work with his hair plastered to his scalp.

"So what's the plan?" I ask Zack.

He crunches down on a lump of granola. "I have to compose a sonata. A symphony." He waves his hand. "A something. It's hard to think about it when Newfield may be coming to an end."

I clatter upstairs to sit on the edge of my bed for a while. What can I do to save us all? Then I smell chocolate two inches from my face.

Steadman, of course.

"How about I show you some pictures?" he says. "You'll be so excited."

Can I just find one secure place to think of how to dismantle a bomb?

Steadman dives onto the bed. "I took one of you and Zack on the roof."

"Nice." I back away from him.

"I have a picture of the bomb, too," he says.

I look up. "You don't have a camera."

He pokes his nose up close. The odor of chocolate is intense. "William's cell phone," he whispers.

"William's cell phone with me on top of St. Ursula's? A picture of the bomb?"

Steadman nods. "And one of the two of you working on Dad's computer."

I'm off the bed as if I've been shot out of a cannon. William will blackmail Zack and me forever.

Steadman jumps off the bed, too. He rocks back and forth on his sneakers. "There's more, but William says he's going to decapitate me if I touch his phone again. Who knows what that means?"

"Did William see the pictures yet?" My mind is racing. William's door is bolted, his windows locked.

Steadman shrugs. He reaches high up into his pajama sleeve. With some effort, he pulls out William's bedroom key.

Hard to believe.

I take the key without a word. Where is William? Downstairs? Outside? Is there enough time to . . .

"William's mixing paint in the basement," Steadman says. "It's a real mess down there."

"Sit here," I tell him. "Don't move. Don't breathe."

"I have to breathe," he says. "And I have to come with you. I know where he hid the phone."

We go down the hall to William's room. I lean over the stairs. I can hear Zack plunking on the cello and Mom singing to Mary. I wish I knew where alpha dog Linny was, but at least William is nowhere in sight. I turn the key in the lock and we're inside.

I leap back against the door.

It's a horror, an absolute horror.

In front of me, a tyrannosaurus is poised to chomp down on—

Zack's head. It really is a painting of Zack. I can tell by the ears and the teeth.

"Great, right?" Steadman says. "William is a genius. Turn around. You're on the other wall."

"No thanks," I say. "Just get the cell phone."

Steadman begins to open drawers. It isn't easy. There's a ton of stuff jammed inside. "I can't remember exactly where . . ." He tosses socks and underwear on the floor.

Someone is clumping up the stairs.

It's William, all right. No one else makes that much noise. Steadman grabs the phone, tosses it to me, and vanishes under the bed.

I slide into the closet as William opens the door. "Hey!" he bellows. "Who made this mess in here?" He's out the door again, probably on his way to find Steadman and decapitate him.

Sometimes Steadman is smarter than I am. He doesn't move. But I take a step out of the closet, the cell phone in my pocket, ready to disappear down the hall.

William turns back and catches me.

We roll around over his underwear. We bump into walls.

Linny screams from the hallway. "Mom, come quick. William is killing Hunter!" She stands in the doorway as Mom barrels up the stairs.

William and I fly apart.

"Hunter's fault," Linny tells Mom.

"How do you know?" I ask.

"I know everything," she says.

She doesn't know about the cell phone, or Steadman under the bed. That gives me a world of satisfaction.

Downstairs Zack is still playing the cello, and in front of me, Mom has her hands on her hips. "Enough," she says in a voice that sounds like Sister Appolonia. She counts in her calming-herself voice. "One, two..."

"Sorry," William says, but not too nicely.

"Sorry," I tell Mom, too, and head for the stairs.

Behind me, Mom is saying, "I can't bear the summers."

I stop. I really love the summers. Poor Mom. She should just sit outside and read a book or something.

And then I hear her say, "Elena Wu can't find Lester's recipe. She always kept it in a special place."

Mom takes a breath and I take one, too.

"I have to compare the new soups with his old recipe," Mom says. "Four, five..."

Linny shakes her head, looking reliable. "It's probably in a book somewhere."

Mom frowns. "It's a good thing I know how it should taste. At least, I think I do."

I rush down to the kitchen. "Never mind the symphony," I tell Zack. "We have a new development."

He drops the cello on the floor and follows me out the door.

We sink down at the side of the house. I pull out William's phone and click on the pictures. In the first, like the ape in *Raw Nature*, Friday morning, seven o'clock, I'm flying from the itchy ball tree toward St. Ursula's roof.

"Wouldn't William like to get his hands on that," I say as Steadman slides in beside us.

"We could sell it to Sarah Yulefski," Zack says. "She could hang it in her living room."

I shudder, thinking of Sarah, but we're on to the next shot: Zack's rear end as he climbs into the steeple.

The third shot is hazy. It was taken from the open door of the firehouse, but it's definitely Lester's huge balloon—the one he blew into town with—all ready for Tinwitty Night.

Zack gasps. This next picture may have captured the worst scene we've ever witnessed. Inside a window, Diglio leans over a body. Man or woman, who knows? There's a look of terror on its face.

It's like a scene from *Terror in a UFO*, Friday night, nine-thirty.

We have to do something fast.

Chapter 14

Zack deletes the photos one by one; then we start down the street. Behind us, almost like a bomb going off, is an explosion of sound.

Splat!

I swivel around, ready to take cover.

A water balloon has hit the sidewalk in front of us. William is hanging out his window.

"Ya, ya!" I yell. "Couldn't hit the side of a barn."

Zack goes further. He holds up William's cell phone. "You nearly drowned your cell phone," he screeches.

William's face turns purple. He disappears from the window.

"He's coming!" Steadman yells.

Don't we know it!

Zack and I fly down the street, swinging Steadman between us, his feet barely touching the ground. We cross Murdock Avenue at a dead run, weaving around parked cars, looking over our shoulders.

William runs like a cheetah. He's half a block behind us

as we cross the library lawn, hop over the NO DOGS ALLOWED sign, and open the double doors that lead inside.

We slide to a stop when we see Mrs. Wu. No one fools around with her.

"Good morning, boys," she says.

We bob our heads. "Looking for . . . ," Zack says, and lets his voice trail off.

Mrs. Wu nods and we tiptoe around the corner. It's a great library with hidden zigzags from A to Z; we know them all.

There's just enough room for the three of us to squeeze into the S-T-U biographies. We sink down, leaning against the shelves, and look up at the picture of Lester Tinwitty.

Lester has more hair on his face than a herd of buffalo.

Outside the window is an excellent view of Vinny's garbage and Dr. Diglio's office.

"Stop breathing so loud," Zack tells me.

"It's not me."

"Not me, either." Steadman pulls out a book, causing a massive collapse. The pile gathers speed as the books clunk off the shelf and onto our laps. One of them looks as if it's falling apart: it's the life story of Lester himself.

But there's really breathing; it comes from behind us, kind of a low snort. I can't pay attention to that right now, though. We hear the library door open. William!

"Hey, Mrs. Wu," he says. "Have you seen my brothers?"

"I do not keep track of everyone in this neighborhood, William," she says. "And your voice is twenty decibels too loud for the reading room."

Zack gives me a silent high five.

Behind us there's that sound. A sneeze? I just have time to think that someone in the stack behind us must have a cold before something explodes through the empty space and grabs my wrist.

"Yeow!"

It's Fred.

Old Lady Campbell looks up from her book. "That dog will be the death of me," she mutters.

He may be the death of me first, I think.

I pull myself free, and he goes after Steadman. Before I can do one thing to save Steadman, Fred dives on top of him and they both land on the floor.

I can hardly look.

But wait.

Fred is slobbering all over Steadman. Licking his face, whining.

Steadman looks up at me. "Fred's my best friend, you know."

But now I hear William's footsteps. Zack and I grab Steadman and we're out the back door.

Diglio's office is right on the other side of the alley. A huge tooth hangs from his window. The tooth is grimy, almost as if it has cavities, and a sparrow's nest is wedged between the roots. You'd think Diglio would clean the thing up to show his interest in teeth.

We lean against the wall and watch William go by out front. He doesn't even look down the alley. Actually, he has the brains of a flea.

We make our way over to Diglio's open window, the tooth screeching above us. It almost sounds like our shopping cart.

Room one is empty, so we move to room two. The window is wide open; dusty blinds rattle in the breeze.

I reach up to steady them in their back-and-forthing. And there's Diglio in a white coat, his four strands of hair combed over his shiny head.

Who is that in his chair? Impossible to see without poking our heads all the way in the window.

Zack sifts through his pocket to find a couple of crumbs and sits Steadman down in front of them. "Just watch," he says. "A herd of ants will be along any minute."

Steadman bends down, his nose almost touching the cement. He looks hypnotized.

That Zack is a genius.

The two of us sink down against the hot brick wall to listen.

"Where does it hurt?" Diglio asks, in a false *I feel your pain* voice.

The answer is garbled. No wonder. It's hard to speak

clearly when Diglio's thick fingers are stretching your lips like rubber bands.

The garble sounds familiar, but it's very noisy around here. Two guys come down the alley, both of them chewing on gyros, shedding lettuce and tomatoes behind them.

It's very distracting.

I inch up to look in the window again. There's a tray of torture instruments, and over the sink is a photograph. I steady the blinds and poke my head in. It's a good thing Diglio's turned the other way.

And look at that photo!

It's Diglio grinning, showing off every single one of his teeth, front to back. Is he saluting someone? Yes. The other guy in the picture looks familiar. Very familiar.

I sink down. I can't believe it. It's the president of the United States.

The president is a spy?

I lean my head against the bricks. What next!

Diglio hums as the garble turns to a moan. After a long moment, he stops and the victim says something that sounds like "I don't like to kill anything."

"Sometimes it just can't be helped," Diglio says. "That's what I tell myself every time I chop off a head."

Zack covers his eyes. "The whole world is going crazy," he says.

The victim goes on. "Cutting them up is the hard part. Their small bodies. Hardly anything is left after—"

"Worrisome," Diglio says.

We lean closer. He said that about my teeth one time, throwing in a lecture about flossing.

But then his phone rings. "Excuse me," he says, and heads toward the other room.

Zack's eyes are as big as Frisbees. "Where do you think they do all this chopping and cutting?"

Diglio's cellar probably looks like a butcher shop.

We crawl along outside to room one to see what Diglio is up to now. Luckily, Steadman is immersed in an ant parade.

Diglio closes the door and reaches into a drawer for a phone. Why does he keep it hidden away? Why is it red? And why, most of all, is he whispering?

Zack and I go up on tiptoes, our chins resting on the sill. Just before Zack knocks over a jar of instruments on the sill, Diglio says, "I'm counting on you, but there isn't much time. Get everything ready. Olyushka."

The crash is spectacular. Diglio jumps a foot and turns. In the other room, the victim screams.

Zack and I grab Steadman again. We run like madmen down the block toward home.

Chapter 15

Mom barbecues outside, a relief because soup entries are bubbling all over the stove, one worse than the other.

Pop chews thoughtfully. "Lester's soup kettle has to be cleaned out," he says.

I know what's coming.

"Get your boots, guys." Pop points to Zack and me.

"What about William?" I say.

"William is helping out in his own way," Mom tells us.

Moments later, Zack and I clump down to the town round. The grandstand is one-third graffiti, but creeping around the edges is a blinding purple paint. An orange solar system explodes over the bleachers.

"Guess who's painting the grandstand," Zack says.

There's something else to look at. In the same orange are huge letters: H.M. ♥ S.Y.

Me and Sarah Yulefski? Horrible.

William's getting back at me. I look away quickly. If only I could change my name.

Zack and I trot up the steps to the soup kettle. I see

we're not alone. Coming down the path are Dr. Diglio and his killer-high-heels wife. He sees me, too, but looks away. It's almost as if he knows that I can almost see into his evil mind. Mrs. Diglio waves. She's afraid of nothing.

And there's Sarah Yulefski standing on the other side of the town round staring at the H.M. ♥ S.Y. sign. It's almost too much to bear.

Zack and I take a huge detour around the other side of the soup kettle, go up the stairs, and look into it. The kettle is almost as big as Pop. We slide the massive cover back inch by inch, both of us pushing. "It sounds like a tomb being opened," Zack says, and I shiver.

We throw in a bucket, a broom, and old rags that look like my last year's underwear. We don't bother with the little rope ladder. We hang on to the rim, then let go, throwing ourselves in, too. We land in candy wrappers, paper plates, and a possum tail, left over from last year's winning entry. Zack tosses it up and over the edge of the kettle.

I look up as a plane from Sturgis Air Force Base soars overhead. Then, with our feet, we swab around, almost like ice skating. We've discovered an echo and treat ourselves to a couple of bloodcurdling screams.

We try doomsday voices next: "Diglio, you're done for, hooodie-hoohoo." We keep our doomsday voices low. He may have X-ray ears.

It's time to finish up and get out of there. But above my head, there's a shadow. The pot cover slides over the top until it's completely black inside. "Hey!" I yell. We're trapped like a pair of chickens on the way to become cacciatore.

I don't know which of us screams louder. It makes the whole thing worse. Our voices twirl around, but they're going nowhere; the cover must be six inches thick. And we don't even have the rope ladder in here with us.

"Don't worry," Zack says at the end of his fortieth yell. "Mom and Pop will take their walk, right around the kettle. We'll be out in no time."

I think of Pop, how strong he is, how smart.

"Right." I cross my fingers. They'll never hear us.

We settle back, our heads against the side. It's hot in here, very hot. I fan myself with both hands.

Something else is happening underneath the pot. We hear clicking and clacking and a thump.

For a moment, we're entirely quiet. Then Zack says, "How did Lester heat the soup, anyway?"

Another thump.

"Someone must have lit a fire underneath." I try to sound calm. But I know exactly what he's thinking. *Could* someone light a fire underneath us? Forget calm. "Yeooooooooow!" I yell.

Zack stamps on the bottom of the pot. "We're in here!" His voice echoes: *"In heeeeeeerrrrre."*

I lean closer to him, even though I can't see an inch in front of me. I do see his eyes, though. Huge. "We can't wait for Mom and Pop," I say. "We'll be bacon before they get here."

"If you stand on my shoulders," Zack says, "maybe you can push the cover off."

And that's what we do. I climb up on Zack. It works better that way because I'm a quarter-inch taller than he is. We slide across the bottom of the pot. Pop would be thrilled. We're cleaning the pot as we're saving our lives.

We're also screaming again, especially Zack. "You're breaking my shoulder bones!" he yells.

I don't answer. My arms are up over my head. For a moment, my fingertips graze the cover. "Hold still, will you, Zack?"

"My toes are burning." He stamps his feet.

"It's your imagination," I say, even though I'm not so sure about that.

I lunge up, thinking of Sister Appolonia, her glasses glinting. *Anything is possible, Hunter Moran. Set your mind to it.* My mind is on it, but I need another half-inch.

We careen back and forth. Zack is losing his balance, I can feel it. "Hold on!" he yells.

I hold on, but it doesn't do any good. We're like a ship in a typhoon.

And then—

Clunk!

I'm tossed off Zack's shoulders and hit the side of the pot. "I'm dead!" I yell.

"Not yet," Zack says. He's breathing, so I must be breathing, too.

"Here's what we're going to try next," he says. "I'm going to stand on your shoulders."

"It won't work."

"But this time, we're both going to stand on tiptoes."

I hear him pulling off his shirt. "I'm fighting for our lives," he says, and wraps the shirt around my shoulders like a cushion.

And I really need it. His feet are large and clunky. I lean against the side of the pot, up on my toes like a ballet dancer. And then we're both sliding, falling, landing on the bottom of the pot.

We're soup.

But no, I hear a voice outside. Whose voice? Who knows?

"Is somebody in there?"

We begin to yell, to pound, to bang our heels against the side.

There's a grating sound. The cover moves slowly, so slowly I'm not even sure it's really edging across the top of the pot.

An inch. Another inch. I see a head. Eyes peering in at us. And teeth.

Sarah Yulefski!

"What are you guys doing in there?" she asks.

"Just cleaning up," I say.

"I could see you needed help," she says, throwing down the rope ladder.

I look up at her braces, festooned with spinach, or maybe broccoli. I open my mouth to say we didn't need any help, but she saved our lives, after all.

"Thanks," I say.

Zack grips the ladder. He's up and over. He reaches down and I grab his hand. I boost myself up and I'm out.

Still breathing.

And there's Diglio disappearing at the far end of the town round.

"My brother's looking for me," Sarah says. "But don't worry, I'll catch up to you."

That's all we need.

"See you tomorrow," Zack says.

"Or maybe when school starts in the fall," I tell her.

Zack nudges me. A pair of fat gray squirrels chase each other across the steps, then under the pot, and out the other side.

"No one was trying to burn us alive," Zack says, reaching for his shirt, which has footprints all over it.

I nod. "Just squirrels."

We head down the path, leaving the broom to fend for itself in the bottom of the pot.

It may even add to the taste of the soup.

Chapter 16

We head across the street. "There's something to think about," I say.

"Shirt's full of grit." Zack scratches away. "Who pushed the cover over the pot?"

We stare at each other. It's very disturbing.

Diglio, of course, trying to warn us.

"But he's lost again," Zack says, pumping his skinny arm. "We are so tough. It's unbelievable."

"Right." And talk about tough, there go Fred and Old Lady Campbell, Fred snapping furiously at a mosquito.

Mom and Pop are almost a block away on their nightly walk. I can almost guess what Zack's thinking. No one knows where we are. Pop will think we've gone home, and, like a miracle, Linny is stuck with Steadman.

Freedom.

"We should go over to Vinny's Vegetables. Get the bomb and bury it somewhere," Zack says.

"Maybe the woods. It'll just blast out a couple of rocks and a lot of dirt."

We snake our way around the town round like a pair of cobras so Mom and Pop, who are getting closer, won't see us.

We're on our way. Vinny's is closed. He doesn't spend one extra minute there for hungry people who need vegetables and much more. The back is lit up like a prison exercise yard. Vinny's showing off his garbage pile to the whole world. It's so high, it almost reaches the top of the fence, a good frog's leap from one to the other.

"No problem," Zack says. "We climb up and jump right in."

We've had a lot of experience climbing and jumping, but never into piles of slimy carrots and broccoli before. In two seconds we find out about this cyclone fence. The holes are made for Mary's size feet, and the whole thing sways as we begin to shinny up.

"It must be ten feet high," Zack says between breaths.

Then we're almost at the top. It's a weird world up there. I can see right into the library, and if I angle my head, I can see the filthy tooth that sways over Diglio's office.

Behind us is a voice. I can't look down, but I know who it is. Of course I do.

"Hi, Hunter," says Sarah Yulefski. "What are you doing up there? Aren't you afraid you'll fall?"

And that's what I do. Right into the arms of Sarah, who has a rim of chocolate around her mouth. At least, I hope it's chocolate. I can't imagine she'd be growing a mustache before she reaches sixth grade.

"Don't worry," she says. "I've got you."

She looks down at me. "So do you just like to climb fences?" she asks.

I begin to shake my head, but I see her smiling with those teeth that would give anyone nightmares. "I saw the sign you painted on the grandstand," she says.

"I never ... It wasn't ..."

"Why didn't you just open the gate?"

What is she talking about? She points. And now I do see. The lock on the fence is gone.

At the same moment, Zack reaches the top; he teeters there for an instant, then sails across into a pile of banana peels. "Yeow!" he yells.

I move away from Sarah Yulefski. "See you." I head for the gate.

Sarah goes along with me.

"See you," I say again, a little louder.

Zack takes giant steps down the hill of rotten vegetables, wiping his sneakers off as he goes. "So long, Sarah," he calls.

"Are you looking for something?" she asks.

We try to ignore her.

"It must be in there pretty deep," Zack says. "We'll have to move a ton of stuff."

He begins to push garbage around. He's filthy and it's getting late. If Mom and Pop get home from their walk before we do, there will be a major inquisition.

"Maybe I can help," Sarah says. "Is it gold? Diamonds? Cash?"

Zack and I look at each other. We could use someone to crawl around in that mess.

"A black box," I say.

"Bomb size," Zack says.

Sarah makes a large square with her hands. "Like this? Rope wrapped around it about a hundred times?"

"That's it," I say. "Dive right in."

Sarah kicks at the fence with one sneaker. "Too late. It's gone."

"It's here," Zack says. "It didn't walk off by itself."

Sarah shakes her head. "No, it walked off with someone else."

I straighten up. "Who?"

"Someone took it. The whole thing was a little sneaky, if you ask me."

"Who?"

She holds up her crossed fingers. "I can't tell. I promised. Crossed fingers three times."

I'd like to say it really is a bomb. I'd like to say this is Sarah Yulefski's chance to save Newfield. But there's no time. Sarah's big brother, Jerry, comes up the street and spots her. "Wait till I get you!" he yells.

He reminds me of William.

Sarah splits. Halfway down the alley she calls back, "I loved the sign."

She disappears and we're left with Vinny's old vegetables and much more.

HERE COMES DAY FOUR....

Tinwitty Night and maybe...

Chapter 17

"Doomsday," Zack says, rolling out of bed. We stare at each other.

"We have to find that bomb," I say.

Zack does that thing with his teeth. "Diglio really means business, locking us up like that. We could have been there until tonight."

I nod, picturing the lid coming off and a pair of skinny skeletons huddled inside.

The door opens and Steadman lands on my bed. "What's that horrible smell?" He high jumps, aiming for the ceiling.

"Tinwitty soup," I say.

With one gigantic jump, Steadman's fingers graze the ceiling, leaving a chocolate print.

Downstairs Mom is clanging pots in the kitchen. The bell will be ringing all morning with last-minute entrants. Bowls of soup, pots of soup, vats of soup, everyone hoping to win the trip to the Ozark Mountains.

Outside the noise is deafening. Seven Guys Over

Seventy are weaving down Murdock Avenue practicing, with horns blaring and drums pounding.

And is that Old Lady Campbell marching behind them? A flimsy-looking scarf and a pair of goggles are looped around her neck. Fred bucks along next to her.

Zack and I throw on shorts and go downstairs for breakfast, with Steadman closer than a shadow. The kitchen is steaming. Mom stands at the counter as Linny dips a spoon into a swampy soup and holds it out to her.

"If only I had Lester's recipe," Mom says, then shudders. "Oh, put this on the back step. There's a rooster head floating on top; its dead eyes are staring at me."

Steadman follows me outside, making google eyes, imitating the rooster, as Pop comes around the side of the house. "Where are the troops?" he calls. "I need help out here."

I back into the house, tiptoe down the hall past William's garish painting, and slide into Mom's bill-paying room. From the kitchen, I hear Mom. "Eureka!" she shouts. "I have a winner."

And there goes Mom's phone. I grab it before the second ring and listen to the static. I whisper-snarl into it, "Yeah?"

"It's Agent Five," the voice says.

I don't believe it. I roll right into "Six."

"By tomorrow the whole thing will be over," the voice says.

Who is it? I know that voice.

But do I really? I can't even tell if it's a boy or a girl, a man or a woman.

"I know it," I say. "The population gone in one blast."

"Six?" the voice asks.

"Mmmm," I say in my deepest, breathiest voice.

Still he/she hesitates.

Could it possibly be Sarah Yulefski? Sarah, a federal agent? Talk about the bottom of the barrel.

"What do you want me to do?" I whisper to keep things going.

A pair of planes from Sturgis Air Force Base zoom overhead. The windows rattle; it sounds as if the roof is ready to cave in. How can I hear?

The caller goes on. "Maybe we'll find the original. I'll search..."

I hear Pop's footsteps. "Is someone in there?" he asks.

I dive behind the desk, cradling the phone in my arms, and stop breathing.

"Are you looking for Hunter?" Linny's voice calls.

Pop doesn't answer. I'm sure he's nodding.

"He's so crafty," Linny says.

Is the doorknob turning? I set the phone back on the desk. But Pop keeps going down the hall. I head for the kitchen in back of him. I need a massive breakfast for what's ahead of me.

Mom is still at the stove. "A perfect Lester Tinwitty soup," she says.

I peer into the huge pot. The soup is the color of Zack's favorite socks, almost purple. Small black things float around on top. And is that an eye? I jump back. Yes, it's an eye.

"Exactly the kind of soup Lester ate on his way here," Mom says. "The same soup he fed the pioneers."

"Whose soup is it?" I ask.

Mom shakes her head; so does reliable Linny. "Top secret," Linny says.

We shovel in what may be our last breakfast as Pop tells us what's going on: the fifty-year-old air force bomber from Sturgis, the fire department truck with its huge ladder, and Lester Tinwitty's balloon are all at the town round.

"That balloon is ready to fall apart." Pop takes a chunk of granola. "Worse, the strings that tie it down look as if they're ready to snap any minute."

But Mom is frowning. "Strange. This soup seems to match the original recipe perfectly." She stares into the pot. "It's almost as if someone found the recipe and—"

"That would be cheating," Linny says.

"More than cheating," Pop says. "More like stealing a free vacation to the Ozark Mountains."

Zack's eyes widen. He gives me a kick under the table. What am I missing? But there's no time for more. Pop turns to Zack. "Better practice. Tonight is your big night."

It's a big night, all right, a night to be blown to smithereens.

Zack scrapes back his chair. He's still looking at me.

"Go," Mom tells him.

Pop leans over the stove. "Want to help me carry the soup?" he asks me.

The pot is huge; the soup is gross. But why not?

"*S-T-U,*" Zack whispers as he goes down the hall.

That would be St. Ursula's.

But he gives me a quick head shake over his shoulder. He knows what I'm thinking. Too bad I haven't a clue about what he's thinking.

Mom shuts the living room door behind him. "Zack needs to concentrate," she says.

Pop and I wrestle the pot onto the shopping cart.

Pop is whistling. "Ah," he says after a moment. "You were going to build a playhouse for Steadman."

I've almost forgotten saying that. I have no idea how to begin. A playhouse. Good grief.

"That was a good thought," Pop says. "We'll do it together. You, me, and Zack."

"I guess so," I say.

"It'll make up for the computer." He begins to whistle again.

I try to think of what to say to that, but I'm speechless. I try a grin.

Is he grinning back? I can't tell. He's too smart for that.

Steadman comes after us in his rabbit pj's, singing the

alphabet song at the top of his lungs. We pass St. Ursula's and get soaked by Father Elmo's sprinkler. "It won't hurt to dilute the soup a little," Pop says.

The town round is like an anthill, everyone getting ready, buzzing and cackling: Seven Guys Over Seventy tooting, and not one on the same note; Sarah Yulefski tuning up her violin; Mr. and Mrs. Wu setting up their frankfurter stand—those homemade hot dogs that taste like dead dogs.

On one side of us looms Lester's old balloon. It's green, and moldy, and billows in the wind. Good thing it isn't going anywhere. I see a small rip in the canvas.

A little farther down is the town's fire engine, with its huge ladder halfway up.

Steadman's almost finished singing. "*P-Q-R . . .*" He stops for a breath. "*T-U-V . . .*"

"*S-T-U,*" I say aloud.

"Sturgis Air Force Base?" Steadman says.

How does he think of these things? But this time he's wrong; this time I get what Zack was trying to tell me. I think about Lester Tinwitty's picture hanging over the *S-T-U* section in the library. It would be just like Mrs. Wu to hide the original recipe there. And from the dentist's office, Diglio could see just what she was doing.

Is that what this is all about? The Diglios stealing a secret recipe just to get to the Ozark Mountains? But why set off a bomb? Maybe half the town owes him money for filling in their cavities. He's into revenge.

That has to be it.

Pop and I hoist the pot of soup to the top of Lester Tin-witty's kettle. "Not much soup for the town to taste."

"Are you kidding?" Pop says. "Who'd want to eat this swill? It's just for the idea of it."

But we all have something to do now: Zack has to create a masterpiece, Steadman has to get dressed, and I have to find a bomb and dismantle it.

Chapter 18

Instead Pop sets me to work on bunting. That's what he calls it. We zigzag along with a huge roll of red-white-and-blue stuff to loop around the telephone poles.

I spend the day tacking, until my fingers have dents in them. Over my head, William splashes orange paint around, finishing up the grandstand.

I hope it's quick-drying paint.

Sarah gets herself right in there, looping and tacking along with me and talking about her contribution to the musical world. "Wait until they hear me," she says. "It will be like Mozart's debut."

At last everything is ready. Pop rolls in the popcorn machine. I hope last year's leftover popcorn is gone. It tasted stale even then.

It's getting dark; lights go on overhead and the signal comes from the fire department: a blast to keep your ears ringing for an hour. Tinwitty Night is ready to begin.

Seven Guys Over Seventy go at it with horns and drums.

It's music that must be seventy years old, but actually not bad if you don't get too close.

People come from all over. Diglio wears his white jacket with I'M THE DOCTOR embroidered on the pocket, and Mrs. Diglio is decked out like a wedding cake in white net. And here comes my buddy Zack with his hair slicked down; he's wearing a new T-shirt and lugging Old Lady Campbell's cello along. He looks like a nervous wreck.

It's really noisy. We have the Seven Guys, Mrs. Wu calling, "Get your hot dogs while they're hot," and Pop yelling, "Popcorn here. Hurry before it's gone."

I keep watching Diglio. He acts as if he's the mayor of the world, shaking everyone's hands with fingers as fat as Mrs. Wu's hot dogs. Imagine, I have to be ready to deck him when the action gets hot.

But for now, the action is the concert. Too bad the pilots at Sturgis Air Force Base have mixed up the timing. They begin their show, twirling and diving over the town round so you can hardly hear Sarah's contribution to the music world. But who could listen for that long, anyway? People begin to yawn as Sarah saws on.

Mom and the other kids are sitting in the grandstand, but Pop has disappeared under the popcorn machine. It must have broken down again. I can see his legs and feet and a bunch of tools scattered around.

Mrs. Diglio's eyes are closed. She's fallen asleep with all

this noise? But then Diglio inches away from the grandstand. He takes a step at a time, looking back, looking guilty?

I search for a weapon. I may have to bash him over the head. I've had a lot of practice with that because of William. But all I see is a stick on the ground. You couldn't even bash a mosquito with it.

Desperately, I motion to Zack. We have to save Newfield. Eyes closed, he's plinking his fingers in the air, playing an imaginary cello, mouthing notes to himself. But Steadman's right there, backing me up.

Everyone claps for Sarah, probably because she's finished at last. And Zack gets to his feet. He looks as if he's a hundred years old. It takes him that long to get to the stand.

Old Lady Campbell is nodding. Her scarf flows. She loops Fred's leash around the edge of the grandstand, pins a note to his collar, and moves away. Her whole seat is orange. Not fast-drying paint after all.

Steadman and I follow Diglio across the round, but we lose sight of him as he circles Tinwitty's balloon.

I hear frothing behind me, but there's no time to look back. It's too bad I don't look at anything that's ahead of me. I trip over the shopping cart that we left there earlier.

I stagger forward and trip over the rope that holds down the balloon. I hear it snap as I hit the next one, and that snaps, too. The balloon basket tips and I fall headlong into it. The frothing thing, Fred, dives in after me.

And then we're rising, spinning, as the planes from Sturgis zoom away. Under me are lights, the grandstand, Zack...

All getting smaller, smaller.

And who's that screaming? I peer over the side of the basket. With one hand Steadman holds on to the trailing rope. Under his arm is the black box.

It's a moment of horror. "Steadman!" I yell, watching his legs dangle. I can't believe it; I can hardly breathe. If something happens to him, it will be the end of everything. "Hold on!" I yell. "Please hold on."

I grab the end of the rope and pull. He's heavier than I thought, and the wind whips around us. But finally I reel him in like a trout, until he collapses into the basket. I put my arms around him. "You're safe," I say.

"I know it," he says back.

So it's Fred, Steadman, and me. And don't forget the black box tied up with rope, a splash of orange paint on one side.

We're all heading for the stratosphere.

Over my head, the rip in the canvas is growing. "Help!" I yell, but everyone is listening to Zack.

We crouch there, watching the world tilt underneath us. Old Lady Campbell throws her cane under the bleachers. She hobbles across the town round.

Fred is trying to bury himself under Steadman. He looks terrified. I don't blame him. I'm terrified, too. We're getting higher by the moment. The wind blows, the canvas flaps, the rip grows.

From behind Steadman, Fred begins to chew on the ropes that cover the bomb box.

And Steadman is loving all of it. "Hey, look!" he shouts. "Fred wants to see the bomb." He grins. "I took the bomb away from William. He thought it was your treasure."

William? Has the world gone crazy?

But I have a quick flash in my mind of Sarah Yulefski at Vinnie's garbage. It was William she saw taking the bomb. William, who must have been spying on us.

Now Diglio looks up. His mouth opens as if he can't believe what he's seeing. "Hey!" he yells. "Hey!"

Zack stops playing, and everyone in the grandstand turns and looks up at us, too. Linny takes a few steps, arms out, crying, *"Hunnnn-terrrrr!"* And is that her friend Becca crying, too?

I'm glad they feel bad for me, because when Pop gets out from under the popcorn machine he's going to banish me to my room for the rest of the summer. And Steadman, too. That is, if any of us are alive. We're sailing toward the woods now. As soon as we're over the trees, I'll lean over the side and hurl the bomb as far away from us as I can.

Fred growls at me from behind Steadman. Gingerly I reach down and take the note from his collar. It's addressed to Zack and me. What's that all about?

But Diglio is doing something really strange. He's

climbed into the fire truck and is zooming toward the woods, his head out, watching us. Wouldn't you know! He still hopes he can capture the bomb.

And what is Old Lady Campbell doing? She's hopped into the old Sturgis Air Force Base plane. For a quick second I think of the pictures in her kitchen drawer. All of them have to do with planes.

But now the propellers whirl and Old Lady Campbell takes off, wearing the goggles, the scarf streaming; she barely misses us as she turns west.

Diglio is underneath us now. He's reaching out and out . . . any minute he's going to crash into the trees that are coming up in front of us. Yeow. And so are we.

That's exactly what happens. Diglio and the balloon hit the same tree at the same time. Leaves and small branches drift into the basket. And Fred climbs into Steadman's lap.

Diglio climbs the ladder toward us as I reach for the bomb. "Don't!" he yells. "Don't—"

But it's too late.

Chapter 19

I shove the bomb over the side of the basket. The box crashes into a branch just below us, the half-chewed rope separates, and the top sails off. What's inside is the most disgusting—

mess—

of dead goldfish.

Five of them.

They fly into the air almost as if they have wings. One lands on me, another on Fred. He opens his mouth and devours it. The rest splatter down onto Diglio's upturned face.

"My poor wife Olyushka's dead fish," Diglio moans.

Olyushka? That's Mrs. Diglio's name? Not the name of a bomb?

But what about Bom/Twin?

Here's something else. As Diglio teeters on the ladder, someone climbs the tree toward us.

I peer down. It's Mom.

"Good work, Five," she tells Diglio as she wedges a foot into the V of a branch above her.

Diglio is Five?

"Thanks, Six," he says.

He grins at us. I have to say his teeth are perfect. "Your mom and I used to call each other agents when we were kids," he says. "I lived at Five Ann Court; she lived at Six."

I close my eyes, trying to make sense of everything. Steadman's photo of Diglio, leaning over a victim whose face is filled with horror. Probably just a patient getting a tooth pulled.

Cheech!

Diglio on the phone. My name, Hunter. He wanted to take care of me. Zack, too, I'm sure.

But *dig*.

I must have said it aloud. "Not digging exactly," Diglio says. "Just another word for searching."

"Searching for what?"

"The original Tinwitty soup recipe," Diglio says.

Over my head, high up, the old plane grinds along.

Mom looks up. "The Bom/Twin," she says.

That's the name of a plane?

Cheech, I tell myself again. And then I think of the revenge note sailing out of the shopping cart. I think of Old Lady Campbell at the library that day, dropping everything. Dropping a note to herself?

Revenge?

Why?

We climb down the fire truck ladder, one after the other, Fred holding on to Steadman.

"It's time to announce the soup winner." Mom sounds a little out of breath.

We head toward the town round like a parade, Steadman and Fred in front. I'm next. Mom and Diglio come up in back of us. I hear them whispering and I slow down, looking up at the stars as if I'm thinking about a constellation or two.

Diglio is talking. "It's fortunate I was there to save these kids. It's all that karate I do. The tae kwon do." He shakes his head. "I have to say, though, your kids are desperadoes. I keep trying to look after them, but it's as hard as looking after their teeth."

I take a quick look back to see Mom give Diglio a St. Dorothy smile. "You're telling me something I don't know?"

In front, Steadman whispers, "What's Diglio talking about, anyway? He didn't save us. We saved ourselves."

Everyone is waiting. Mom climbs the steps to stand in front of Lester Tinwitty's soup kettle. She waves her hand at the winning pot of soup on top.

The crowd ducks as the plane with Old Lady Campbell dives down and loops over the town round.

Zack comes up to me as Mom clears her throat. "Not a bad sonata," he says. "Thought it up as I went along." He slaps my shoulder. "Too bad I missed the balloon ride. But I saw two fighter jets streak after Old Lady Campbell. I wonder if they'll catch her."

And there's Mom talking now; her voice is squeaky. "The winner is . . ."

I move forward to hear her better. The note from Old Lady Campbell crackles in my pocket.

There's a drumroll from one of the Seven Guys Over Seventy. And Mom calls, "Vincent Moochmore!"

Who is that? Then it comes to me. Vinny's Vegetables and Much More.

Vinny bounds up the steps. "Thank you!" he yells. "I always wanted to win."

Wait a minute. I remember spying on Diglio's office, the familiar voice I heard. Yes, it was Vinny, and he was talking about cutting up small bodies. Sardines?

Zack leans over. "From the top of Vinny's garbage pile, you can see right into the library window."

I nodded. "He must have seen Mrs. Wu putting the original recipe into Lester's book in the S-T-U section."

Zack's eyes widen. "He stole the original recipe."

"Sneaky!" Steadman yells at the top of his lungs. "Vinny's a thief."

"I should have figured it out myself," Diglio says.

And Mom and Mrs. Wu look at Vinny with suspicion. "Well?" Mom asks him.

He reaches into his pocket and pulls out a yellowed paper. "I've never won anything in my life. I've never been to the Ozarks." He sighs. "And I found this original recipe stuck in a book."

"I thought your soup was too good to be true." Mom stands up straight. "Vincent Moochmore, you're disqualified."

"Disgraceful," Mrs. Wu says as she snatches the original away from him.

Head down, Vinny sneaks out of the town round, and I sink down against the grandstand. My back sticks to the paint. I pull out Old Lady Campbell's note.

But Mom is down the steps and holds out her hand. "I'll take that," she says, and begins to read.

I look over her shoulder.

Diglio appears. He looks over her shoulder, too.

Dear Zack and Hunter,

You'll be thrilled to know I'm leaving Fred for you as a gift. I've taken the old Bom/Twin plane. It's my revenge.

I was the first one to fly this plane years ago, and I was the one who drew up the Bom/Twin plans with Leon Bomson.

I will contact Sturgis Air Force Base at some point. If they want it back, they'll have to pay. (Plenty.)

In the meantime, I'm off to see the world.

Love,

Constance Campbell

P.S. I waited to take off so I could hear Zack play his music. Maybe he should take up another instrument next year.

"Well, Six," Diglio says, "Tinwitty Day is over for another year. Tomorrow, Olyushka and I will take a little vacation. I'm not going to think about kids in a balloon and dead fish hanging in trees for at least a week."

"You deserve it," Mom says.

William is right behind us. "I thought you and Steadman were goners in that balloon," he says. "It was the worst moment of my life."

Zack and I look at each other. Sometimes William surprises us.

"I guess I shouldn't have put Lester Tinwitty's soup cover over you," William goes on.

"You did that?" I'd like to bash him, but he looks really sorry. Instead we wend our way to the hot dog stand. The hot dogs are rock hard, but we don't need to starve to death. Fred follows, high-stepping along with Steadman, looking like *Best Friend Buddy*, Tuesdays, three-thirty.

We eat three hot dogs each, and get one for Pop, who is still working on the popcorn machine. Good thing he didn't see what went on with the balloon.

I cross my fingers. With Pop you never know.

There's another drumroll. The new winner is Old Lady Campbell. She didn't even need to win. She's probably heading for the Ozarks anyway.

IT'S ANOTHER DAY, AND NOT A MYSTERY IN SIGHT.

Instead...

Chapter 20

I feel the sun against my closed eyes. I think of the beach, I think of...

What's that noise outside? Banging. Hammering. Yelling.

"Ignore it," Zack mutters. "Go back to sleep. It's summer. Even Pop is on vacation. And now that Old Lady Campbell will probably end up in prison, I don't have to take music lessons anymore. She can teach Bach to the rest of the inmates instead."

There's more banging. "Yeow!" Pop yells.

"He's hit his thumb with the hammer," Zack says as we climb out of our beds.

"Hunter! Zack!" Pop shouts.

"I knew we'd be involved somehow," Zack says.

From the hall window, I peer into the yard. It's a nightmare out there. Boards all over the place. Pop's rusty tools. A keg of nails.

Zack leans over my shoulder. At the same time, Pop looks up and sees us. "Time's a-wasting," he calls, cradling his thumb.

It comes to me in one horrible flash. It comes to Zack, too.

"You're building my playhouse today," Steadman says from the stairs. "Pop says it was your idea. Thanks, Hunter."

"Yeah, thanks a lot, Hunter," Zack says.

We clump down the stairs, take a fistful of granola and a slug of orange juice.

"There's no help for it," Zack says through a mouthful of granola. "We'll have to spend the day out there, sun pouring down, dying of thirst, like *Doom in the Desert*, Tuesday mornings, seven-thirty."

"You're right," I say. "We'll be holding boards while Pop hammers his fingers to pieces."

Outside, Pop acts like we're building the Taj Mahal. Zack has to measure every piece of wood. I have to sort through the nails to find non-rusty ones.

Zack is right. It's about two hundred degrees, and by noon, only one wall is finished.

"What do you say, men?" Pop says. "We don't need lunch, right?"

After a while, the rest of the walls go up, and the roof. Pop cuts in a door, and Zack gets the idea to add a window.

It's looking good.

And now there's a little shade. Mom makes a quick trip outside with lemonade and sandwiches, and Linny's baked sugar cookies. All you have to do is saw the burned parts off with your teeth.

It's late afternoon by the time we're finished. Steadman hops around, just missing our feet. "I'm going to move right in when I'm ten," he says.

At last we step back. Pop's arm goes around the two of us. "It's great to spend a day working with your sons," he says. "And there's no one I'd rather work with than you two. I'm a lucky guy."

Actually it's been a great day.

I look up at Pop and move closer. "We're lucky too," I say, and Zack nods.

We really are.

Pop grins at us. "Look who's coming."

I don't want to look. I hear the voice. It's Sarah Yulefski.

I turn. She's wearing a tan bathing suit, the color of her teeth. "Want to swim in my pool?" she asks Zack and me.

Pop gives my shoulder a squeeze.

We're steaming hot.

Why not?

"Wait till I get my bathing suit," I say.

Yee-ha! It's summer.